RUTH RENDELL

Classic British crime fiction is the best in the world -- and Ruth Rendell is crime fiction at its very best. Ingenious and meticulous plots, subtle and penetrating characterizations, beguiling storylines and wry observations have all combined to put her at the very top of her craft.

Her first novel, *From Doon with Death,* appeared in 1964, and since then her reputation and readership has grown steadily with each new book. She has now received five major awards for her work: two Edgars from the Mystery Writers of America; the Crime Writers' Gold Dagger Award for 1976's best crime novel for *A Demon in My View*; the Arts Council National Book Award for Genre Fiction in 1981 for *Lake of Darkness*; and in 1985 the Crime Writers' Silver Dagger Award for *The Tree of Hands*.

Ruth Rendell's novels have received outstanding reviews

'Ruth Rendell is really first-class . . . a natural story-teller' *Times Literary Supplement*

'The appearance of any novel by Ruth Rendell is a cause for celebration' *Spectator*

'Ruth Rendell's superb crime novels make her my favourite to inherit the title Queen of Crime' Graham Lord, *Sunday Express*

'Britain's new Queen of Crime' *Daily Mirror*

D0951755

Also in Arrow by Ruth Rendell

RUTH RENDELL

SOME LIE AND SOME DIE

ARROW BOOKS

Arrow Books Limited
62–65 Chandos Place, London WC2N 4NW

An imprint of Century Hutchinson Limited

London Melbourne Sydney Auckland
Johannesburg and agencies throughout
the world

First published by Hutchinson 1973
Arrow edition 1974
Reprinted 1979, 1980, 1985 and 1986 (twice)

Printed and bound in Great Britain
by Anchor Brendon Ltd, Tiptree, Essex

ISBN 0 09 909280 8

To my son, Simon Rendell, who goes
to festivals, and my cousin,
Michael Richards, who wrote the
song, this book is dedicated with
love and gratitude.

Let-me-believe

I don't miss her smile or the flowers,
I don't eclipse distance or hours,
I don't kiss the wind or the showers,
I miss her, can't kiss her with lips that were ours.

So come by, come nigh,
    come try and tell why
    some sigh, some cry,
    some lie and some die.

Remember me and my life-without-life,
Come once more to be my wife,
Come today before I grieve,
Enter the web of let-me-believe.

So come by, come nigh, etc.

The house will be as if it were ours,
She'll fill the void with love-scented flowers,
She'll sit with me in the fast-fading light,
Then my dream will sift into night.

So come by, come nigh, etc.

Now she's gone in the harsh light of day,
When she'll return the night would not say,
And I am left to vision the time
When once more she'll come and be mine.

So come by, come nigh,
    come try and tell why
    some sigh, some cry,
    some lie and some die.

(Zeno Vedast's song from the 'Let-me-believe' L.P.
and the 'Sundays Album', issued by Galaphone Ltd
and obtainable from good record shops everywhere.)

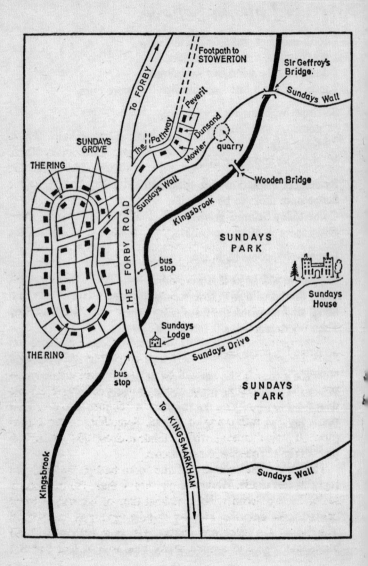

1

'But why here? Why do they have to come here? There must be thousands of places all over this country where they could go without doing anyone any harm. The Highlands for instance. Dartmoor. I don't see why they have to come here.'

Detective Inspector Michael Burden had made these remarks, or remarks very much like them, every day for the past month. But this time his voice held a note which had not been there before, a note of bitter bewilderment. The prospect had been bad enough. The reality was now unreeling itself some thirty feet below him in Kingsmarkham High Street and he opened the window to get a better—or a more devastating —look.

'There must be thousands of them, all coming up from Station Road. And this is only a small percentage when you consider how many more will be using other means of transport. It's an invasion. God, there's a dirty-looking great big one coming now. You know what it reminds me of? That poem my Pat was doing at school. Something about a pied piper. If "pied" means what I think it does, that customer's pied all right. You should see his coat.'

The only other occupant of the room had so far made no reply to this tirade. He was a big, heavy man, the inspector's senior by two decades, being at that time of life when people hesitated to describe him as middle-aged and considered 'elderly' as the more apt epithet. His face had never been handsome. Age and a very nearly total loss of hair had not improved its pouchy outlines, but an expression that was not so much easy-going as tolerant of everything but intolerance, redeemed it and made it almost attractive. He was sitting at his rosewood desk, trying to compose a directive on crime prevention, and now, giving an impatient shake of his head, he threw down his pen.

'Anyone not in the know,' said Chief Inspector Wexford, 'would think you were talking about rats.' He pushed back his chair and got up. 'A plague of rats,' he said. 'Why can't you expand your mind a bit? They're only a bunch of kids come to enjoy themselves.'

'You'll tell a different tale when we get car-burning and shop-lifting and decent citizens beaten up and—and Hell's Angels.'

'Maybe. Wait till the time comes. Here, let me have a look.'

Burden shifted grudgingly from his point of vantage and allowed Wexford a few inches of window. It was early afternoon of a perfect summer's day, June the tenth. The High Street was busy as it always was on a Friday, cars pulling into and out of parking places, women pushing prams. Striped shop awnings were down to protect shoppers from an almost Mediterranean sun, and outside the Dragon workmen sat on benches drinking beer. But it was not these people who had attracted Burden's attention. They watched the influx as avidly as he and in some cases with as much hostility.

They were pouring across the road towards the bus stop by the Baptist church, a stream of boys and girls with packs on their backs and transistors swinging from their hands. Cars, which had pulled up at the zebra crossing to let them pass, hooted in protest, but they were as ineffectual as the waves of the Red Sea against the Children of Israel. On they came, not thousands perhaps, but a couple of hundred, laughing and jostling each other, singing. One of them, a boy in a tee-shirt printed with the face of Che Guevara, poked out his tongue at an angry motorist and raised two fingers.

10

Mostly they wore jeans. Not long since they had been at school—some still were—and they had protested hotly at the enforced wearing of uniforms. And yet now they had their own, voluntarily assumed, the uniform of denims and shirts, long hair and, in some cases, bare feet. But there were those among them making a total bid for freedom from conventional clothes, the girl in red bikini top and dirty ankle-length satin skirt, her companion sweating but happy in black leather. Towering above the rest walked the boy Burden had particularly singled out. He was a magnificent tall Negro whose hair was a burnished black bush and who had covered his bronze body from neck to ankles in a black and white pony-skin coat.

'And that's only the beginning, sir,' said Burden when he thought Wexford had had time enough to take it all in. 'They'll be coming all night and all tomorrow. Why are you looking like that? As if you'd—well, lost something?'

'I have. My youth. I'd like to be one of them. I'd like to be swinging along out there, off to the pop festival. Wouldn't *you*?'

'No, frankly, I wouldn't. I'm sure I never would have. Those young people are going to cause a lot of trouble, make a hell of a noise and ruin the weekend for all those unfortunate citizens who live on the Sundays estate. Heaven help them, that's all I can say.' Like most people who make that remark, Burden had a lot more to say and said it. 'My parents brought me up to be considerate of the feelings of others and I'm very glad they did. A trip to the local hop on a Saturday night, maybe, and a few drinks, but to take over God knows how many acres of parkland just to indulge my tastes at the expense of others! I wouldn't have wanted it. I'd have thought I hadn't achieved enough to deserve it.'

Wexford made the noise the Victorians wrote as 'Pshaw!' 'Just because you're so bloody virtuous it doesn't mean there aren't going to be any more cakes and ale. I suppose you'll stop that boy of yours going up there?'

11

'I've told him he can go to Sundays tomorrow evening for two hours just to hear this Zeno Vedast, but he's got to be in by eleven. I'm not having him camp there. He's only just fifteen. Zeno Vedast! That's not the name his godfathers and godmothers gave him at his baptism, you can bet your life. Jim Bloggs, more like. He comes from round here, they say. Thank God he didn't stay. I don't understand this craze for pop music. Why can't John play classical records?'

'Like his dad, eh? Sit at home getting a kick out of Mahler? Oh, come off it, Mike.'

Burden said sulkily, 'Well, I admit pop music's not my style. None of this is.'

'Your scene, Mike, your scene. Let's get the jargon right. We're pigs and fuzz as it is. We don't have to be square as well. Anyway, I'm sick of being an onlooker. Shall we get up there?'

'What, now? We'll have to be there tomorrow when the fighting and the burning starts.'

'I'm going now. You do as you like. Just one thing, Mike. Remember the words of another Puritan—"Bethink ye, bethink ye, in the bowels of Christ, that ye may be mistaken." '

Where the Regency mansion now stands a house called Sundays has stood since the Norman Conquest. Why Sundays? No one knows. Probably the name has nothing to do with the Sabbath Day; probably—and this is the general belief—it derives from the name of the man who built the first house, Sir Geffroy Beauvoir de Saint Dieu.

Once the Sundays lands extended from Kingsmarkham to Forby and beyond, but gradually fields and woodlands were sold off, and now the house has only a small garden and a park of a few acres. In the eyes of the preservationists Sundays is irretrievably spoilt. Its tall cedars remain and its avenue of hornbeams, the overgrown quarry is still untouched, but the Italian garden is gone. Martin Silk, the present owner,

12

grows mushrooms in the orangery, and the view is ruined by the newly built Sundays estate.

The Forby road skirts the park and bisects the estate. It is along here that the Forby bus runs four times a day, halting at the Sundays request stop which is outside the park gates. Wexford and Burden pulled in to a lay-by and watched the first of the young pilgrims tumble out of the two-thirty bus and hump their baggage over to the gates. These were open and on the lodge steps stood Martin Silk with half a dozen helpers ready to examine tickets. Wexford got out of the car and read the poster which was pasted over one of the gates: *The Sundays Scene, June 11th and 12th, Zeno Vadast, Betti Ho, The Verb To Be, Greatheart, The Acid, Emmanuel Ellerman.* As the busload went through and passed into the hornbeam avenue, he went up to Silk.

'Everything O.K., Mr Silk?'

Silk was a small man in late middle age with shoulder-length grey hair and the figure—at any rate, until you looked closely or saw him walk—of a boy of twenty. He was rich, eccentric, one of those people who cannot bear to relinquish their youth. 'Of course it's O.K.,' Silk said abruptly. He had no time for his own contemporaries. 'Everything will be fine if we're left alone.'

He stepped aside, turning on a big smile, to take tickets from half a dozen boys whose slogan-painted Dormobile, pink, orange and purple, had come to a stop by the lodge.

'Welcome, friends, to Sundays. Pitch your tents where you like. First come, first served. You can park the truck up by the house.'

Burden, who had joined them, watched the Dormobile career rather wildly up the avenue, music braying from its open windows.

'I hope you know what you're doing,' he said dourly. 'Beats me why you want to do it.'

'I want to do it, Inspector, because I love young people. I

13

love their music. They've been hounded out of the Isle of Wight. No one wants them. I do. This festival is going to cost thousands and a good deal of it will come out of my pocket. I've had to sell another bit of land to raise money and people can say what they like about that.'

Burden said hotly, 'The preservationists will have plenty to say, Mr Silk. The older residents don't want all this new building. Planning permission can be rescinded. you know.'

Seeing Silk's face grow red with anger, Wexford intervened.

'We all hope the festival's going to be a success. I know I do. I'm told Betti Ho's arriving in her own helicopter tomorrow afternoon. Is that a fact?' When Silk, somewhat appeased, nodded, he went on: 'We want to keep the Hell's Angels out and try to keep trouble down to a minimum. Above all, we don't want violence, bikes set on fire and so on, the kind of thing they had at Weeley. I want to address the crowd before the concert starts, so maybe you'll allow me the use of your platform tomorrow evening. Shall we say six?'

'I don't mind as long as you don't antagonise people.' Silk greeted a group of girls, beaming on them, complimenting them on their ankle-length, vaguely Victorian gowns, approving the guitars which they wore slung from their shoulders. They giggled. At him, rather than with him, Wexford thought privately, but the encounter had the effect of putting Silk in a better temper. When the girls had wandered off into the park he said quite graciously to the policemen, 'D'you want to have a look round?'

'If you please,' said Wexford.

The encampment was to be sited on the left-hand side of the avenue where, under the limes and the cedars, a small herd of Friesians usually grazed. The cattle had been removed to pasture behind the house and the first of the tents were already up. In the midst of the park a stage had been erected, faced by arc-lamps. Wexford, who generally deplored armoured fences, was glad that Sundays park was enclosed by a spiked wall to keep what Burden called 'undesirable elements' out. At only one point was the wall broken and this was at the side of the quarry, a deep semicircular fissure in the chalk at the Forby end. The two policemen walked up to the house, stood on the terrace and surveyed the scene.

A mobile shop selling soft drinks, crisps and chocolate had already been parked in the avenue, and a queue of hungry youth had formed alongside it. The stronger-minded were staking claims to desirable sites and banging in tent pegs. Through the gates came a thin but steady stream of new arrivals, on foot, in cars and on motor-cycles. Wexford jerked his head in the direction of the quarry and walked down the steps.

The lucky ones—those who had taken a day off work or missed a college lecture—had got there in the morning and established their camps. A boy in a Moroccan burnous was frying sausages over a calor-gas burner while his friends sat cross-legged beside him, entertaining him vocally and on a guitar. The Kingsbrook flows through Sundays park, dipping under the Forby Road and meandering between willows and alders close to the wall. It had already become a bathing place. Several campers were splashing about in the water, the girls in bras and panties, the boys in the black scants that serve as underpants or swimming trunks. Crossing the little wooden bridge, Burden looked the other way. He kept his eyes so determinedly averted that he almost fell over a couple who lay embraced in the long grass. Wexford laughed.

' "And thou," ' he said, ' "what needest with thy tribe's black tents who hast the red pavilion of my heart?" There's going to be a lot of that going on, Mike, so you'd best get used to it. Letts'll have to put a couple of men on that quarry if we don't want gate-crashers.'

'I don't know,' said Burden. 'You couldn't get a motor-bike in that way.' He added viciously: 'Personally, I couldn't care less who gets in free to Silk's bloody festival as long as they don't make trouble.'

On the Sundays side the chalk slope fell away unwalled; on the other it was rather feebly protected by broken chestnut paling and barbed wire. Beyond the paling, beyond a narrow strip of grass, the gardens of three houses in The Pathway were visible. Each had a tall new fence with its own gate. Wexford looked down into the quarry. It was about twenty feet deep, its sides overgrown with brambles and honeysuckle and wild roses. The roses were in full bloom, thousands of flat shell-pink blossoms showing against the dark shrubby growth and the golden blaze of gorse. Here and there rose the slim silver trunks of birches. In the quarry depths was a little natural lawn of turf scattered with harebells. One of the flowers seemed to spiral up into the air, and then Wexford saw it was not a flower at all but a butterfly, a Chalkhill Blue, harebell-coloured, azure-winged.

'Pity they had to build those houses. It rather spoils things, doesn't it?'

Burden nodded. 'These days,' he said, 'I sometimes think you have to go about with your eyes half-closed or a permanent crick in your neck.'

'It'll still be lovely at night, though, especially if there's a moon. I'm looking forward to hearing Betti Ho. She sings those anti-pollution ballads, and if there's anything we do agree on, Mike, it's stopping polution. You'll like Miss Ho. I must admit I want to hear this Vedast bloke do his stuff, too.'

'I get enough of him at home,' said Burden gloomily. 'John has his sickly love stuff churning out night and day.'

They turned back and walked along under the willows. A boy in the river splashed Wexford, wetting his trouser legs, and Burden shouted angrily at him, but Wexford only laughed.

2

'On the whole, they're behaving themselves very well.'

This remark was delivered by Inspector Burden on a note of incredulous astonishment as he and Wexford stood (in the words of Keats) on a little rounded hill, surveying from this eminence the *jeunesse dorée* beneath. It was Saturday night, late evening rather, the sky an inverted bowl of soft violet-blue in which the moon hung like a pearl, surrounded by bright galaxies. The light from these stars was as intense as it could be, but still insufficient, and the platform on which their own stars performed was dazzlingly illuminated, the clusters of arc-lamps like so many man-made moons.

The tents were empty, for their occupants sat or lay on the grass, blue now and pearling with dew, and the bright, bizarre clothes of this audience were muted by the moonlight, natural and artificial, to sombre tints of sapphire and smoke. And their hair was silvered, not by time but by night and the natural light of night-time. The calor-gas stoves had been extinguished, but some people had lit fires and from these arose slender spires, threads of blue melting into the deeper blue of the upper air. The whole encampment was blue-coloured, azure, jade where the parkland met the sky, tinted here and there like the plumage of a kingfisher, and the recumbent bodies of the *aficionados* were numberless dark blue shadows.

'How many, d'you reckon?' Wexford asked.

'Seventy or eighty thousand. They're not making much noise.'

17

> 'The moan of doves in immemorial elms
> And murmuring of innumerable bees,'

quoted Wexford.

'Yes, maybe I shouldn't have thought of them as rats. They're more like bees, a swarm of bees.'

The soft buzz of conversation had broken out after Betti Ho had left the stage. Wexford couldn't sort out a single word from it, but from the concentrated intense atmosphere, the sense of total accord and quietly impassioned indignation, he knew they were speaking of the songs they had just heard and were agreeing with their sentiments.

The little Chinese girl, as pretty and delicate and clean as a flower, had sung of tides of filth, of poison, of encroaching doom. It had been strange to hear such things from such lips, strange in the clear purity of this night, and yet he knew, as they all knew, that the tides were there and the poison, the ugliness of waste and the squalor of indifference. She had been called back to sing once more their favourite, the ballad of the disappearing butterflies, and she had sung it through the blue plumes of their woodsmoke while the Kingsbrook chattered a soft accompaniment.

During the songs Burden had been seen to nod in vehement endorsement, but now he was darting quick glances here and there among the prone, murmuring crowd. At last he spotted his son with a group of other schoolboys, and he relaxed. But it was Wexford who noted the small additions John and his friends had made to their dress, the little tent they had put up, so that they would appear to conform with the crowd and not be stamped as mere local tyros, day boys and not experienced boarders.

Burden swatted at a gnat which had alighted on his wrist and at the same time caught sight of his watch.

'Vedast ought to be on soon,' he said. 'As soon as he's finished I'm going to collar John and send him straight home.'

'Spoilsport.'

The inspector was about to make a retort to this when the buzzing of the crowd suddenly increased in volume, rising to a roar of excited approval. People got up, stood, or moved nearer to the stage. The atmosphere seemed to grow tense.

'Here he comes,' said Wexford.

Zeno Vedast was announced by the disc jockey who was compèring the festival as one who needed no introduction, and when he advanced out of the shadows on to the platform the noise from the audience became one concentrated yell of joy. Rather different, Wexford thought wryly, from the chorus of 'Off, off, off . . . !' which had been their response to his own well-thought-out speech. He had been proud of that speech, tolerant and accommodating as it was, just a few words to assure them there would be no interference with their liberty, provided they behaved with restraint.

The police didn't want to spoil the festival, he had said, inserting a light joke; all they wanted was for the fans to be happy, to co-operate and not to annoy each other or the residents of Kingsmarkham. But it hadn't gone down at all well. He was a policeman and that was enough. 'Off, off, off,' they had shouted and 'Out, fuzz, out.' He hadn't been at all nervous but he had wondered what next. There hadn't been any next. Happily, law-abidingly, they were doing their own thing, listening to their own music in the blue and opalescent night.

Now they were roaring for Vedast and at him. The sound of their voices, their rhythmically clapping hands, their drumming feet, assailed him in a tide and seemed to wash over him as might a wave of floodwater. And he stood still in the white ambience, receiving the tide of tribute, his head bent, his bright hair hanging half over his face like a hood of silver cloth.

Then, suddenly, he flung back his head and held up one

hand. The roar died, the clamour softened to a patter, dwindled into silence. Out of the silence a girl's voice called, 'Zeno, we love you!' He smiled. Someone came up to the stage and handed him a bulbous stringed instrument. He struck a single, low, pulsating note from it, a note which had an esoteric meaning for the crowd, for a gentle sigh arose from it, a murmur of satisfaction. They knew what he was going to sing first, that single note had told them and, after a rustle of contentment, a ripple of happiness that seemed to travel through all eighty thousand of them, they settled down to listen to what that note had betokened.

'It's called "Let-me-believe",' whispered Burden. 'John's got it on an L.P.' He added rather gloomily: 'We know it better than the National Anthem in our house.'

'I don't know it,' said Wexford.

Vedast struck the single note again and began immediately to sing. The song was about love; about, as far as Wexford could gather, a girl going to her lover's or her husband's house and not loving him enough or something and things going wrong. A not unfamiliar theme. Vedast sang in a clear low voice, face deadpan, but they didn't let him get beyond the first line. They roared and drummed again; again he stood silent with head bent; again he lifted his head and struck the note. This time they let him complete it, interrupting only with a buzzing murmur of appreciation when his voice rose an octave for the second verse.

'Remember me and my life-without-life,
Come once more to be my wife,
Come today before I grieve,
Enter the web of let-me-believe . . .'

The melody was that of a folk-song, catchy, tuneful, melancholy, as befitted the lyric and the tender beauty of the night. And the voice suited it utterly, an untrained, clear tenor. Vedast seemed to have perfect pitch. His face was bony with a big nose and wide mobile mouth, the skin pallid in the moonlight, the eyes very pale in colour, perhaps a light hazel or a glaucous green. The long, almost skeletal, fingers drew not an accompaniment proper, not a tune, from the strings, but a series of isolated vibrant notes that seemed to twang into Wexford's brain and make his head swim.

> 'So come by, come nigh,
> come try and tell why
> some sigh, some cry,
> some lie and some die.'

When he had finished he waited for the tide to roar over him again, and it came, pounding from and through the crowd, a river of acclaim. He stood limply, bathing in the applause, until three musicians joined him on the stage and the first chords from their instruments cut into the tumult. Vedast sang another ballad, this time about children at a fair, and then another love-song. Although he hadn't gyrated or thrown himself about, his chest, bare and bead-hung, glistened with sweat. At the end of the third song he again stood almost limply, sensitively, as if his whole heart and soul were exposed to the audience, the clapping, the roaring, flagellating him. Why then, Wexford wondered, did he feel that, for all the man's intensity, his simplicity, his earnestness, the impression he gave was not one of sincerity? Perhaps it was just that he was getting old and cynical, inclined to suspect all entertainers of having one eye on the publicity and the other on the money.

But he hadn't thought that of Betti Ho. He had preferred her childlike bawling and her righteous anger. Still, he must be wrong. To judge from the noise the crowd was making as their idol left the stage, he was alone in his opinion, apart, of course, from Burden, who had been determined from the start to like nothing and who was already off in search of John.

'God, when I think of my own youth,' said Wexford as they strolled towards an open space where a van had arrived selling hot dogs. 'When I think of the prevalent attitude that it was somehow *wrong* to be young. We couldn't wait to be older so that we could compete with the old superior ruling people. They used to say, "You wouldn't understand at your age, you're too young." Now it's the young people who know everything, who make the fashions of speech and manners and clothes, and the old ones who are too old to understand.'

'Hum,' said Burden.

'We're two nations again now. Not so much the rich and the poor as the young and the old. Want a hot dog?'

'May as well.' Burden joined the queue, coldly disregarding the hostile glances he got, and bought two hot dogs from a boy in a striped apron. 'Thanks very much.'

'Thank *you*, dad,' said the boy.

Wexford laughed gleefully. 'You poor old dodderer,' he said. 'I hope your ancient teeth are up to eating this thing. How d'you like being my contemporary?' He pushed through the queue towards a stand selling soft drinks. 'Excuse me!'

'Mind who you're shoving, grandad,' said a girl.

Now it was Burden's turn to laugh. 'Contemporary? We're three nations, young, old and middle and always will be. Shall we go and look at the quarry?'

There was to be no more live music for an hour. People had got down to cooking or buying their evening meals in earnest now. A strong smell of frying rose and little wisps of smoke. Already boys and girls could be seen dressed in red and yellow tee-shirts, stamped with the words 'Sundays Scene' on chest and sleeves. The arc-lamps' range wasn't great enough to reach the river, but as the night deepened, the moon had grown very bright. No one was bathing in the clear shallow water, but bathers had left evidence behind them, trunks and bras and jeans spread over the parapet of the bridge to dry.

They walked round the rim of the quarry, brambles catching at their ankles, the tiny, newly formed berries of the wayfarer's tree occasionally tapping their faces, berries which felt like ice-cold glass beads.

The place seemed to be entirely empty, but on the estate side the barbed wire had been cut and broken down. The twisted metal gleamed bright silver in the moonlight. Neither Wexford nor Burden could remember if the wire had been like that yesterday. It didn't seem important. They strolled along, not speaking, enjoying the loveliness of the night, the scent of meadowsweet, the gentle, keening music coming from far away.

Suddenly a gate opened in the fence of the last house in The Pathway and a man came out. He was a tall man with a hard, handsome face and he looked cross.

'Are you by any chance running this'—he sought for an appropriate word—'this rave-up?'

'I beg your pardon?' said Wexford.

The man said rudely, 'You look too superannuated to be audience.'

'We're police officers. Is anything wrong?'

'*Wrong?* Yes, plenty's wrong. My name's Peveril. I live there.' He pointed back at the house whose garden gate he had come from. 'There's been an unholy racket going on for twenty-four hours now and the pace has hotted up revoltingly in the past three. I've been attempting to work, but that's quite impossible. What are you going to do about it?'

'Nothing, Mr Peveril, provided no one breaks the law.' Wexford put his head on one side. 'I can't hear anything at present, apart from a distant hum.'

'Then you must be going deaf. The trees muffle the noise down here. I don't know what use you think you're being here. You ought to hear it from my studio.'

'You were warned in plenty of time, sir. It'll all be over tomorrow. We did advise people who live near Sundays and

23

who felt apprehensive about the festival to notify us of their intention and go away for the weekend.'

'Yes, and have their homes broken into by teenage layabouts. Experience ought to have taught me not to expect decency from you people. You're not even in the thick of it.' Peveril went back into his garden and banged the gate.

'We ought to have asked him if he'd seen any interlopers,' said Burden, grinning.

'Everyone's an interloper to him.'

Wexford sniffed the air appreciatively. He lived in country air, he was used to it. For years he had never troubled to savour it, but he did now, not being sure how much longer it would last. The night was bringing its humidity, little mists lying low on the turf, wisps of whiteness drifting over the quarry walls. A hare started from a tangle of dog roses, stared at them briefly and fled across the wide silver meadow, gawky legs flying.

'Listen,' Wexford whispered. 'The nightingale . . .'

But Burden wasn't listening. He had stopped to glance into the brake from which the hare had come, had looked further down, done a double take, and turned, his face red.

'Look at that! It really is a bit much. Apart from being— well, disgusting, it happens to be against the law. This, after all, is a public place.'

The couple hadn't been visible from the Sundays side. They lay in a small declivity on the floor of the quarry where the lawn dipped to form a grassy basin about the size of a double bed. Burden had spoken in his normal voice, some twenty feet above their heads, but the sound hadn't disturbed the boy and girl, and Wexford recalled how Kinsey had said that in these circumstances a gun could be fired in the vicinity and the report pass unheard.

They were making love. They were both naked, eighteen or nineteen years old, and of an absolute physical perfection. Across the boy's long arched back the fern-like leaves of the mountain ash which sheltered them scattered a lightly moving pattern of feathery black shadows. They made no sound at all. They were entirely engrossed in each other. And yet they seemed at the same time to be one with their surroundings, as if this setting had been made for them by some kindly god who had prepared it and waited yearningly for the lovers to come and make it complete.

The boy's hair was long, curly and golden, the girl's black and spread, her face cut crystal in the moonlight. Wexford watched them. He could not take his eyes away. There was nothing of voyeurism in the fascination they had for him and he felt no erotic stimulus. A cold atavistic chill invaded him, a kind of primeval awe. Bathed by the moonlight, enfolded by the violet night, they were Adam and Eve, Venus and Adonis, a man and woman alone at the beginning of the world. Silver flesh entwined, encanopied by an ever-moving, shivering embroidery of leaf shadows, they were so beautiful and their beauty so agonising, that Wexford felt enter into him that true panic, the pressure of procreating, urgent nature, that is the presence of the god.

He shivered. He whispered to Burden, as if parodying the other's words, 'Come away. This is a private place.'

They wouldn't have heard him if he had shouted, any more than they heard the sudden throb which thundered from the stage and then the thumping, yelling, screaming tumult as The Verb To Be broke into song.

3

There had been no trouble. A party of Hell's Angels had come to Sundays gates and been turned away. The walls were not high enough to keep them out but they kept out their bikes. A tent had caught fire. There was no question of arson. Someone had lit a fire too close to the canvas and Silk had housed the dispossessed owners in one of his spare bedrooms.

The singing went on most of the night, the keening swell, the thunderous roars, of it audible as far away as Forby, and calls from outraged residents—Peveril among them—came steadily into Kingsmarkham police station. By dawn all was silent and most people asleep. The fires had been stamped out and the arc-lamps switched off as the sun came up to shine on Sundays through a golden haze.

The day promised to be less hot, but it was still very warm, warm enough for the campers to bathe in the Kingsbrook and queue up afterwards for ice-cream. By noon the vendors of food and drink and souvenirs had parked their vans all the way up the avenue. The canned music and the music made by little amateur groups ceased and Emmanuel Ellerman opened the second day of the concert with his hit song, 'High Tide'. The mist which had lain close to the ground at dawn had risen to lie as a blanket of cloud through which the sun gleamed palely. It was sultry and the atmosphere made people breathless.

Burden's son John had been allowed to return and hear Zeno Vedast sing for the last time. He kept out of his father's way, embarrassed in this society to have a policeman for a

26

parent. Burden sniffed the air suspiciously as he and Wexford walked about the encampment.

'That smell is pot.'

'We've got enough to think about here without indulging in drug swoops,' said Wexford. 'The Chief Constable says to turn a blind eye unless we see anyone actually high and whooping about or jumping over the quarry because he's full of acid. I wish I could appreciate the noise those musicians are making but it's no good, I can't. I'm too bloody old. They've finished. I wonder who's next?'

'They all sound the same to me.' Burden kept looking for his son, fearing perhaps that he was being corrupted into taking drugs, making love or growing his hair. 'And they all look the same.'

'Do stop fretting about that boy of yours. That's not him you're looking at, anyway. I saw him go off to the hamburger stall just now. Hear that noise? That'll be Betti Ho's helicopter come to fetch her away.'

The bright yellow helicopter, like a gigantic insect in a horror film, hovered and spun and finally plopped into the field behind the house. The two policemen watched it come down and then joined the stream of people passing through the gate into the field. The Chinese singer wore a yellow dress —to match her aircraft?—and her black hair in a pigtail.

'What money she must get,' said Burden. 'I won't say *earn*.'

'She makes people think. She does a lot of good. I'd rather she had it than some of these politicians. There's your John, come to see the take-off. Now, don't go to him. Leave him alone. He's enjoying himself.'

'I wasn't going to. I'm not so daft I don't realise he doesn't want to know me here. There's Vedast. God, it's like the end of a state visit.'

Wexford didn't think it was much like that. A thousand or so of the fans had massed round the helicopter while Betti Ho stood in the midst of a circle of others, talking to Vedast who wore black jeans and whose chest was still bare. There was another girl with them and Vedast had his arm round her waist. Wexford moved closer to get a better look at her, for of all the striking, bizarre and strangely dressed people he had seen since Friday, she was the most fantastic.

She was nearly as tall as Vedast and good-looking in the flashy, highly coloured fashion of a beauty queen. It seemed to Wexford impossible that anyone could naturally possess so much hair, a frothy, bouffant mane of ice-blonde hair that bubbled all over her head and flowed nearly to her waist. Her figure was perfect. He told himself that it would need to be not to look ridiculous in skin-tight vest and hot pants of knitted string, principal-boy boots, thigh-high in gilt leather. From where he stood, twenty yards from her, he could see her eyelashes and see too that she wore tiny rainbow brilliants studded on to her eyelids.

'I wonder who that is?' he said to Burden.

'She's called Nell Tate,' said Burden surprisingly. 'Married to Vedast's road manager.'

'Looks as if she ought to be married to Vedast. How do *you* know, anyway?'

'How d'you think, sir? John told me. Sometimes I wish pop was an O Level subject, I can tell you.'

Wexford laughed. He could hardly take his eyes off the girl, and this was not because she attracted him or even because he admired her looks—he didn't. What intrigued him was contemplating for a moment the life her appearance advertised, a life and way of life utterly remote, he imagined, from anything he had ever known or, come to that, anything the majority of these fans had ever known. It was said that Vedast was a local boy made good. Where did she come from? What strange ladder had she climbed to find herself here and now the cynosure of so many eyes, embraced in public by the darling of the 'scene'?

Vedast withdrew his arm and kissed Betti Ho on both cheeks. It was the continental statesman's salute that has become the 'in' thing for a certain élite. Betti turned to Nell Tate and they too kissed. Then the Chinese girl climbed into her helicopter and the doors were closed..

'Things'll break up soon,' said Burden. 'What time is it?'

'Half four. The air's very heavy. Going to be a storm.'

'I wouldn't like to be in that thing in a storm.'

The aircraft buzzed and whirred and rose. Betti Ho leaned out and waved a yellow silk arm. The fans began to drift back towards Sundays park, drawn by the sound of amplified guitars. The Greatheart, a three-man group, had taken the stage. Burden, listening to them, began to show his first signs of approval since the beginning of the concert. The Greatheart made a speciality of singing parodies of wartime hits, but Burden didn't yet know they were parodies and a half-sentimental, half-suspicious smile twitched his lips.

Martin Silk was sitting on a camp-stool by the ashes of a dead fire talking to the boy in the magpie coat. It was too warm and humid to wear a jacket, let alone a fur coat, but the boy hadn't taken it off, as far as Wexford had noticed, since his arrival. Perhaps his dark bronze skin was accustomed to more tropical skies.

'Not a spot of trouble, you see,' said Silk, looking up.

'I wouldn't quite say that. There was that fire. Someone's reported a stolen bike and the bloke selling tee-shirts has had a hell of a lot pinched.'

'It's quite O.K. to nick things from *entrepreneurs*,' said the magpie boy in a mild, soft voice.

'In your philosophy, maybe. If and when it ever becomes the law of the land I'll go along with you.'

'It will, man, it will. Come the revolution.'

Wexford hadn't actually heard anyone speak seriously of the promised revolution as a foreseeable thing since he was himself a teenager in the early thirties. Apparently they were still on the same old kick. 'But then,' he said, 'there won't be any *entrepreneurs*, will there?'

The magpie boy made no reply but merely smiled very kindly. 'Louis,' said Silk proudly, 'is reading philosophy at the University of the South. He has a remarkable political theory of his own. He is quite prepared to go to prison for his beliefs.'

'Well, he won't for his beliefs,' said Wexford. 'Not, that is, unless he breaches the peace with them.'

'Louis is the eldest son of a paramount chief. One day Louis Mbowele will be a name to be reckoned with in the emerging African states.'

'I shouldn't be at all surprised,' said Wexford sincerely. In his mind's eye he could see future headlines, blood, disaster, tyranny, and all well meant. 'Philosophy doctorate, political theory, British prison—he'll soon have all the qualifications. Good luck. Remember me when thou comest into thy kingdom.'

'Peace be with you,' said the African gravely.

Burden was standing with Superintendent Letts of the uniformed branch.

'Nearly all over, Reg,' said Letts.

'Yes, I don't want to be mean, but I'd like it soon to be over. All done and trouble-free.'

'Before the storm comes too. It'll be hell getting this lot off the park in a downpour.'

Above the roof of Sundays house the sky had deepened to indigo. And the house itself was bathed in livid light, that wan, spectral light that gleams under cloud canopies before a storm. The hornbeams in the avenue, stolid, conical trees, were too stocky to sway much in the rising breeze, but the low broomlike branches of the cedars had begun to sweep and sigh against the turf and, up by the house, the conifers shivered.

It was a hot wind, though, and when Zeno Vedast walked on to the stage he was still half-naked. He sang the 'Let-me-believe' ballad again to a silent crowd made tense by the stifling, thick air.

Wexford, who had once more wandered a little apart so that he was close by the scaffolding of the stage, found himself standing beside Nell Tate. Vedast was singing unaccompanied this time and she held his mandoline or ocarina or whatever it was. There was nothing exceptional in the fact that her eyes were fixed on the singer. So were seventy or eighty thousand other pairs of eyes. But whereas the rest showed enthusiasm, admiration, critical appreciation, hers were hungrily intense. Her gleaming mulberry-coloured lips were parted and she held her head slightly back in a yearning, swan-like curve. A little bored by the song, Wexford amused himself in watching her and then, suddenly, she turned and looked him full in the face.

He was shocked. Her expression was tragic, despairing, as if she had been and was for ever to be bitterly deprived of what she most wanted. Misery showed through the plastered biscuit make-up, the rosy blusher, the green and blue eyelid paint, and showed in spite of the absurd twinkling brilliants stuck about her eyes. He wondered why. She was older than he had thought at first but still only about twenty-eight. Was she in love with Vedast and unable to have him? That seemed improbable, for when Vedast had finished his first song he stepped over to the edge of the stage, squatted down and, in taking the stringed thing from Nell's hand, kissed her impulsively, but slowly and passionately, on the mouth. Vedast began singing again and now Wexford saw that she was looking calmer, the glittering lids closed briefly over her eyes.

'Is that the lot?' he asked, going back to Burden. 'I mean, is the concert over?'

Burden slipped unprotestingly into his role as pop expert, though a less likely or less enthusiastic authority could hardly have been found. 'Two more songs from The Greatheart,' he said, 'and then we can all go home. Some are going already. They only waited to hear the Naked Ape.'

'Fighting words, Mike, sacrilege. I thought he was rather good. There goes that pink and orange van. It's got graffiti all over it—did you see?—and someone's written on one of the doors "This truck also available in paperback".'

The tents were coming down. Gas burners and kettles and tins of instant coffee were being thrust into kit bags, and a barefoot girl wandered vaguely about looking among the heaps of litter for the shoes she had discarded twenty-four hours before. The future leader of an emerging African state had abandoned polemics for the more prosaic pursuit of rolling up his sleeping bag. Martin Silk strolled among them, smiling with regal benignity at his young guests and rather malicious triumph at Wexford.

'You can't help feeling sorry for those Greatheart people, singing their guts out to an audience who couldn't care less. They must know they only stayed for Vedast.'

Wexford's words went unheard. 'There they are,' said Burden, 'that girl and her boy friend, the ones we saw last night. Coming straight from the quarry. Well, their little honeymoon's over. And they've had a row by the look of them or been bitten by something. It's always said there are adders on Sundays land.'

'You'd like that, wouldn't you?' Wexford snapped. 'That'd be a suitable retribution for doing what comes naturally in the Garden of Eden.' The girl and the boy showed no sign of having quarrelled, nor did either of them seem disabled. They were holding hands and running like Olympic sprinters. In a dirty and tattered version of the tee-shirt-jeans uniform, their long hair wind-blown, they had lost their primeval beauty of the night before. The magic and the wonder was all gone. They were just an ordinary young couple running, breathless and—frightened. Wexford took a step in their direction, suddenly concerned.

They stopped dead in front of him. The girl's face was white, her breath laboured and choked. 'You're police, aren't you?' the boy said before Wexford could speak. 'Could you come, please? Come and see what . . .'

'In the quarry,' the girl said throatily. 'Oh, *please*. It was such a shock. There's a girl lying in the quarry and she's—she's dead. Ever so dead. Her face is—blood—horrible . . . Oh *God*!' She threw herself into the boy's arms and sobbed.

4

She was screaming hysterically.

'You tell me,' Wexford said to the boy.

'We went to the quarry about ten minutes ago.' He talked jerkily, stammering. 'I—we—I'm with a party and Rosie's with a party and—and we shan't see each other again for a month. We wanted to be private but it's still daylight and we looked for somewhere we wouldn't be seen. Oh, Rosie, don't. Stop crying. Can't you *do something*?'

A crowd had gathered around them. Wexford spoke to a capable-looking girl. 'Take her into one of the tents and make some tea. Make it hot and strong. One of you others, find Mr Silk and see if he's got any brandy. Come along now. She'll tell you all about it. She'll want to.'

Rosie let forth a shriek. The other girl, justifying Wexford's faith in her, slapped one of the wet white cheeks. Rosie gagged and stared.

'That's better,' said Wexford. 'Into the tent with you. You'll be all right when you've had a hot drink.' He went back to the boy. 'What's your name?'

'Daniel. Daniel Somers.'

'You found a girl's body in the quarry?' Suddenly The Greatheart burst into song. 'God, I wish we could have a bit of hush. Where did you find it?'

'Under some bushes—well, sort of trees—on the side where the wire is.' Daniel shuddered, opening his eyes wide. 'There were—flies,' he said. 'Her face was all over blood and it was sort of dried and there were flies—*crawling*.'

'Come and show me.'

'Do I have to?'

'It won't take long,' Wexford said gently. 'You don't have to look at her again, only show us where she is.'

By now a fear that something had gone badly wrong had flurried the encampment on the side where they were standing, rumour 'stuffing the ears of men with false reports'. People came out of tents to stare, others raised themselves on one elbow from the ground, briefly deaf to The Greatheart. A low buzz of conversation broke out as boys and girls asked each other if this was the beginning of a drug swoop.

Daniel Somers, his face as white, his eyes as aghast as his girl friend's, seemed anxious now to get the whole thing over. He scrambled down the chalk slope and the policemen followed him in less gainly fashion. As yet there was nothing to see, nothing alarming. Under the louring grey sky, thick, purplish, not a blue rift showing, the quarry grass seemed a brighter, more livid green. Light, obliquely and strangely filtered under cloud rims, gave a vivid glow to the white faces of the wild roses and the silver undersides of birch leaves, lifting and shivering in the wind. On the little lawn the harebells shook like real bells ringing without sound.

Daniel hesitated a few feet from where a young birch grew out of a dense, man-high tangle of honeysuckle and dogwood. He shivered, himself near to hysteria.

'In there.' He pointed. 'I didn't touch her.'

Wexford nodded.

'You get back to Rosie now.'

The bushes had no thorns and were easily lifted. They surrounded the root of the tree like the fabric of a tent belling about its pole. Under them, half-curled around the root, lay the girl's body. It was somewhat in the position of a foetus, knees bent, arms folded so that the hands met under the chin.

Even Wexford's strong stomach lurched when he saw the face or what had been a face. It was a broken mass, encrusted with black blood and blacker flies which swarmed and buzzed sluggishly as the leafy covering was disturbed. Blood was in the hair too, streaking the yellow, fibrous mass, matting it in places into hard knots. And blood was probably on the dark red dress, but its material, the colour of coagulated blood, had absorbed and negatived it.

The Greatheart were still performing.

'A girl's been murdered,' Wexford said to Silk. 'You must get this lot off the stage. Let me have a microphone.'

The crowd murmured angrily as the musicians broke off in the middle of a song and retreated. The murmur grew more menacing when Wexford appeared in their place. He held up one hand. It had no effect.

'Quiet, please. I must have quiet.'

'Off, off, off!' they shouted.

All right. They could have it straight and see if that silenced them. 'A girl has been murdered,' he said, pitching his voice loud. 'Her body is in the quarry.' The voices died and he got the silence he wanted. 'Thank you. We don't yet know who she is. No one is to leave Sundays until I give permission. Understood?' They said nothing. He felt a deep pity for them, their festival spoiled, their eager young faces now cold and shocked. 'If anyone has missed a member of their party, a blonde girl in a red dress, will he or she please inform me?'

Silk behaved rather as if Wexford himself had killed the girl and put her in his quarry. 'Everything was going so well,' he moaned. 'Why did this have to happen? You'll see, it'll be another lever in the hands of the fuddy-duddies who want to suppress all free activity and gag young people. You see if I'm not right.' He gazed distractedly skywards at the grey massy clouds which had rolled out of the west.

Wexford turned from him to speak to a boy who touched his arm and said, 'There was a girl in our party who's disappeared. No one's seen her since this morning. We thought she'd gone home. She wasn't enjoying herself much.'

'How was she dressed?'

The boy considered and said, 'Jeans, I think, and a green top.'

'Fair hair? Mauve tights and shoes?'

'God, no. She's dark and she wasn't wearing anything like that.'

'It isn't she,' said Wexford.

The rain was coming. He had a brief nightmarish vision of rain descending in torrents on the encampment, turning the trodden grass into seas of mud, beating on the fragile tents. And all the while, throughout the night certainly, he and every policeman he could get hold of would have to interrogate wet, unhappy and perhaps panicky teenagers.

The photographers had come. He saw their car bumping over the hard turf and stop at the wooden bridge. Once she had been photographed, he could move her and perhaps begin the business of identification. He felt a dash of cold water on his hand as the first drops of rain fell.

'I've been wondering if we could get them all into the house,' said Silk.

Eighty thousand people into one house? On the other hand, it was a big house...

'Not possible. Don't think of it.'

Behind him a girl cleared her throat to attract his attention. Two girls stood there, one of them holding a black velvet coat.

'Yes?' he said quickly.

'We haven't seen our friend since last night. She left her coat in the tent and just went off. We can't find her or her boy friend, and I thought—we thought...'

'That she might be the girl we found? Describe her, please.'

'She's eighteen. Very dark hair, very pretty. She's wearing black jeans. Oh, it isn't her, is it? She's called Rosie and her boy friend...'

'Is Daniel.' While the girl stared at him, round-eyed, marvelling at this omniscience, he said, 'Rosie's all right.' He pointed. 'She's over there, in that tent.'

'Thanks. God, we were really scared.'

How much more of this was there to be, he wondered, before he had to say yes, yes, it sounds like her? Then he saw Dr Crocker, lean, trim and energetic, stalking towards him. The police doctor wore a white raincoat and carried an umbrella as well as his bag.

'I've been away for the weekend, Reg, taking your people's advice. I thought I was going to keep clear of all this. What's it about?'

'Didn't they tell you?'

'No, only that I was wanted.'

'There's a dead girl in the quarry.'

'Is there, by God? One of *them*?' Crocker pointed vaguely into the crowd.

'I don't know. Come and see.'

The rain was falling lightly, intermittently, the way rain does after a drought and before a deluge, as if each drop was being squeezed painfully out. Three police cars had succeeded in negotiating the rough ground and were parked at the quarry edge. In the quarry itself the photographers had completed their work, the undergrowth had been cut away and a tarpaulin canopy erected to screen the body from view. In spite of this, a crowd of boys and girls squatted or lolled all round the quarry, speculating among themselves, their eyes wide.

'Get back to your tents, the lot of you,' Wexford said. 'You'll get wet and you won't see anything.' Slowly, they began to move. 'Come on now. Ghoulishness is for ignorant old people. Your generation is supposed to be above this sort of thing.'

That did it. One or two of them grinned sheepishly. By the time Wexford and the doctor had scrambled down on to the little lawn—the harebells trodden to a mush—the sightseers had dispersed. Crocker knelt by the body and examined it.

'She's been dead at least five days.'

Wexford felt himself relax with relief.

'She was dead before the festival started,' said Crocker, 'and she wasn't a teenager. I'd say at least twenty-seven, maybe thirty.'

Under the canopy the flies were thick and noisy. Wexford rolled the body on to its side, revealing a large handbag of mauve patent leather which lay beneath it. Handbag, shoes and tights matched each other and clashed with the dark red dress. He opened the bag, spilling the contents on to a sheet of plastic. An envelope addressed to Miss Dawn Stonor, 23 Philimede Gardens, London, S.W.5, fell out. There was a letter inside it addressed from Lower Road, Kingsmarkham:

Dear Dawn, I will be glad to see you Monday but I suppose it will be one of your flying visits and you won't condesend to stop the night. Granma has had one of her bad turns but is all right again now. I got the mauve slacks and blouse from the cleaners that you left there and you can take it away with you. They charged 65 p. which I will be glad of. See you Monday. Love, Mum.

He noted the illiteracies, the badly formed writing. Something else in the letter struck a chord in his mind, but he could think about that later. The main thing was that she had been easily and rapidly identified. 'Have the body removed,' he said to Sergeant Martin, 'and then I want the quarry searched.'

There was blood on his hand, fresh blood. How could that have come from a body five days dead? He looked again and saw that it hadn't. The blood was his own, flowing from a small wound near the base of his thumb.

'Broken glass everywhere,' he said wonderingly.

'Have you only just noticed?' Crocker gave a harsh, humourless laugh. 'You needn't bother to search for a weapon.'

They had come gaily and noisily, erupting from cars and trains and buses, arriving on a summer's day to hear music and bringing their own music with them. They left downcast, in silence, trudging through the rain. Most of them had had no more than a dozen hours of sleep throughout the weekend. Their faces were shocked and dirty and pale.

No one ran. There was no horseplay. They dismantled their wet tents, shouldered their baggage, leaving behind them greyish-white mountain ranges of rubbish. Moving towards the gates in long ragged files, they looked like refugees leaving a place of disaster. Daniel walked with Rosie, one arm embracing her, the other shouldering a rolled tent which bumped against his khaki pack. Louis Mbowele passed through the gates without looking up from the book he was reading. They chewed sweets, passed wine bottles from hand to hand in silence, indifferent in their saddened freemasonry as to who paid or who drank. Huddled together, they lit cigarettes, sheltering match flames from the downpour.

Lightning split the sky over Stowerton and the thunder rolled, grumbling in the west. From fast-travelling clouds, blue and black and roaring grey, the rain cascaded, sweeping people and their belongings into the avenue like so much debris buffeted by the tide. The cedars lifted their black arms, sleeved in spiky foliage, and slapped them, rattling, up and down on what had been turf. It was turf no longer. Thousand upon thousand of strong young feet had shaved the grass to stubble, to final scorched aridity. The rain fell on to acres of brown desert.

Someone had abandoned a torn tent, a red canvas tent that bounded in the wind like a huge drowning butterfly until it became waterlogged and collapsed against the footings of the stage. The river began to fill, carrying with it as it plunged under the Forby Road a bobbing flotsam of paper, cans, transistor batteries and lost shoes.

5

With the rain came a kind of false night, a streaming, early twilight. It drove everyone indoors, everyone, that is, but the departing young people who trudged through the downpour into Kingsmarkham. Soaked and shivering, the long processions came on towards the buses, towards the station. Some stayed behind on the Forby Road, hoping to hitch, doggedly resigned when cars passed without stopping, when motorists, put off by their draggled clothes and their long wet hair, rejected them.

They invaded the centre of the town, queueing for any bus that might come, forming dispirited lines that stretched the length of the High Street. A conglomeration of youth filled the centre, but the outskirts, the back streets, were deserted. In Lower Road where all the doors and windows were shut, every curtain drawn, rain drumming on rows of pavement-parked cars, it might have been the depths of winter. Only the roses in the front gardens of these squat red-brick council houses, the drooping foliage on cherry trees, showed that there should have been sunshine, that it was a June evening.

Number fifteen was a house just like its neighbours, a similar Dorothy Perkins trailing over the front door, its acid pink flowers clashing with ochreish red brick, similar white net curtains, draped crosswise like the bodice of a negligé, across its windows. A scaffolding of television aerials sprouted from its single chimney and juddered in the gale.

Wexford went slowly up the path. The rain was falling so heavily that he had to put up his umbrella even for this short distance from the car to the front door. He hated having to question the bereaved, hated himself for intruding on their grief and for feeling, if not showing, impatience when memories overcame them and tears silenced them. He knew now that Dawn Stonor had had no father. It was a woman in the barren country of deep middle age, alone and perhaps utterly broken, he had to interview. He tapped softly on the door.

Detective Polly Davies let him in.

'How is she, Polly?'

'She's O.K., sir. There wasn't much love lost between mother and daughter, as far as I can see. Dawn hadn't lived at home for ten years.'

Dreadful to feel relief at a lack of love . . . 'I'll talk to her now.'

Mrs Stonor had been driven to the mortuary and home again in a police car. Still wearing her coat, her red straw hat on the arm of her chair, she sat in the living room, drinking tea. She was a big, florid-faced woman of fifty-five with bad varicose veins, her swollen feet crushed into court shoes.

'Do you feel up to giving me some information, Mrs Stonor? I'm afraid this has been a bad shock for you.'

'What d'you want to know?' She spoke abruptly in a shrill, harsh voice. 'I can't tell you why she was in that quarry. Made a proper mess of her, didn't he?'

Wexford wasn't shocked. He knew that in most people there is something sado-masochistic, and even the newly-bereaved have an apparently ghoulish need to dwell with pleasurable horror on the injuries inflicted on dead relatives. Whether or not they express these feelings depends on their degree of cultivated repression rather than on grief.

'Who was "he", Mrs Stonor?'

She shrugged. 'Some man. There was always some man.'

'What did she do for a living?'

'Waitress in a club. Place called the Townsman up in

London, up West somewhere. I never went there.' Mrs Stonor gave him a lowering, aggressive look. 'It's for men. The girls get themselves up in daft costumes like bathing suits with skirts, showing off all they've got. "Disgusting!" I said to her. "Don't you tell me about it, I don't want to know." Her dad would have turned in his grave if he'd known what she did.'

'She came here on Monday?'

'That's right.' She took off her coat. He saw that she was heavily built, rigidly corseted. Her face was set in grim, peevish lines, and it was hard to tell whether it was more grim and peevish than usual. 'You wouldn't find a decent girl going to that quarry with a man,' she said. 'Had he done anything to her?'

The question was grotesque between people who had seen for themselves, but he knew what she meant. 'There was no sexual assault and intercourse hadn't taken place.'

She flushed darkly. He thought she was going to protest at his fairly blunt way of speaking but instead she rushed into an account of what he wanted to know. 'She came down by train, the one that gets in at half past eleven. I'd got her dinner for her, a bit of steak. She liked that.' The harsh voice wavered a little. 'She liked her bit of steak, did Dawn. Then we chatted a bit. We hadn't really got nothing in common any more.'

'Can you tell me what you talked about?'

'Nothing about *men*, if that's what you mean. She was fed-up on account of some little kid in the train had wiped his sticky fingers down her dress. It was a new dress, one of them minis, and it showed all her legs. I said she'd have to change it and she did.'

'She put on the dark red dress she was found in?'

'No, she never. That wasn't hers. I don't know where that come from. There was a mauve thing she had here as I'd fetched from the cleaners for her—they call them trouser suits —and she put that on. She was wearing mauve shoes so it looked all right. Well, like I said, we chatted a bit and she

43

went up to see her gran—that's my mother as lives with me—and then Dawn went off to catch the four-fifteen train. Left here just before four.'

Wexford looked thoughtful. 'You thought she was going straight back to London?'

'Of course I did. She said so. She said, I've got to be in the club by seven. She took the blue dress with her in a bag and she said she'd have to run not to miss her train.'

'Two more things, Mrs Stonor, and then I'll leave you in peace. I'd like you to describe the trouser suit, if you would.'

'Very showy, it was. More like pyjamas than something you'd wear in the street. There was slacks, sort of flared, and a kind of tunic. It was mauve nylon stuff with a bit of darker mauve round the sleeves and the bottom of the tunic. Dawn liked to dress flashy.'

'Have you a photograph of her?'

Mrs Stonor gave him a suspicious glare. 'What, got up in them clothes?'

'No. Any photograph.'

'There was a photo she sent me for Christmas. Funny idea giving your mum a photo of yourself for Christmas, I thought. You can have that if you like.'

The photograph, a studio portrait, was brought. It had never been framed and, from its pristine condition, Wexford supposed that it had never been shown with pride to Mrs Stonor's friends but kept since its arrival in a drawer. Dawn had been a heavy-featured, rather coarse-looking girl, who wore thick make-up. The blonde hair was piled into puffs and ringlets, a massy structure reminding him of the head-dresses of eighteenth-century belles or perhaps of actresses playing such parts. She wore a blue silk evening gown, very low-cut and showing a great deal of fleshy bosom and shoulder.

Mrs Stonor eyed it irritably, peevishly, and Wexford could see that it would have been a disappointing gift for a mother of her type. Dawn had been twenty-eight. To have met with maternal favour, the picture should have shown not only a daughter but grandchildren, a wedding ring on those stiffly posed fingers, and behind the group the outline of a semi-detached house, well kept-up and bought on a mortgage.

He felt a stirring of pity for this mother who was a mother no longer, a flash of sympathy which was dissipated at once when she said as he was leaving:

'About that trouser suit...'

'Yes?'

'It was more or less new. She only bought it back in the winter. I mean, I know a lady who'd give me five pounds for that.'

Wexford gave her a narrow glance. He tried not to show his distaste.

'We don't know what's become of it, Mrs Stonor. Perhaps the lady would like the shoes and the bag. You can have them in due course.'

The exodus continued. By now it was dark, a windswept, starless night, the rain falling relentlessly. Wexford drove back to the Sundays estate where, on both sides of the Forby road, police cars cruised along the streets or stood parked in lakes of trembling black water. Presently Burden found him and got into the car beside him.

'Well? Anything startling?'

'Nothing much, sir. Nobody remembers seeing a girl in a red dress down here during the week. But last Monday afternoon one woman from Sundays Grove, a Mrs Lorna Clarke, says she saw a blonde girl, answering Dawn's description, but wearing a...'

'Mauve trouser suit?'

'That's right! So it was her? I thought it must be from Mrs Clarke talking about mauve shoes and a mauve bag. Where did the red dress come from then?'

Wexford shook his head. 'It's beginning to look as if she

died on Monday. She left her mother's house just before four that afternoon. When and where did your Mrs Clarke see her?'

'She got off the five-twenty-five bus from Kingsmarkham. Mrs Clarke saw her get off the bus and cross the road towards The Pathway. A few minutes later someone else saw her in The Pathway.'

'Which backs on to the quarry. Go on.'

'There are only five houses in The Pathway, two bungalows and three proper houses. If you remember, they didn't do any more building down there. People made a fuss about it and the ministry reversed the decision to grant planning permission. She was next seen by a woman who lives in the last house.'

'Not the wife of that bloke who came out making a to-do on Saturday night?'

Burden nodded. 'A Mrs Peveril, sir. They're both at home all day. He's a graphic designer, works at home. His wife says she saw a blonde girl in mauve go down the road at five-thirty and enter the public footpath that goes across the fields to Stowerton. She gave a very detailed description of the trouser suit, the shoes and the bag. But, of course, I couldn't be sure it was Dawn. I couldn't understand her being dressed in mauve. Mrs Peveril says the girl was holding a brown carrier bag.'

'Mm-hm. It certainly was Dawn. She changed out of a blue dress into the mauve thing and it was obviously the blue one she was carrying in the bag. She seems to have gone in for a lot of clothes changing, doesn't she? I wonder why. No other help from The Pathway?'

'No one else saw her. Each of the bungalows has only one occupant and they were both out at the relevant time. Miss Mowler's a retired district nurse and she was out on Monday till eight. Dunsand—he's a lecturer at the University of the South, philosophy or something—didn't get home from work till after half past six. I can't find anyone else who saw her on

Monday or at any other time. My guess is she picked up some bloke and made a date to meet him between Sundays and Stowerton that evening.'

'Ye-es. I expect that's it. She left her mother at four and she must have caught the five-twelve bus. There are only two buses going to Forby in the afternoon, as you know. What did she do in that spare hour and ten minutes? We'll have to find out if anyone saw her in the High Street. There's the London angle too, but I've already got wheels moving there.'

'D'you want to see Mrs Peveril?'

'Not now, Mike. I doubt if we can make much progress tonight. I'll let them finish the house-to-house. They may get something more. She may have been seen later. I don't want to speculate at this stage.'

Burden left the car and, throwing his raincoat over his head, plunged off through the rain. Wexford turned the car, moving off in low gear through the torrents, the steady downpour, glancing once at Sundays where the last dispirited stragglers were leaving the park.

6

By the morning it had been established that Mrs Margaret Peveril of number five, The Pathway, was very probably the last person to have seen Dawn Stonor alive. On Monday, June sixth, Dawn had entered the pathfields at five-thirty and disappeared. By nine Wexford and Burden were back in The Pathway. By nine also an emergency interview room had been set up in the Baptist church hall where Sergeant Martin and a team of detectives waited to talk to anyone who might have seen Dawn on the previous Monday afternoon. The photograph had been blown up to poster size ready to jog memories, and another photograph prepared, this time of Polly Davies wearing a blonde wig and dressed in clothes resembling as nearly as possible Mrs Stonor's description of the mauve suit.

The rain had stopped during the night and the town and its environs looked washed, battered, wrung out to dry. All the summer warmth had gone with the storm, leaving a cloud-splashed sourly blue sky, a high sharp wind and mid-winter temperatures.

At Sundays Martin Silk was burning litter, the accumulated detritus of eighty thousand people's weekend. A row of fires blazed just behind the wall and the wind blew acrid white smoke in clouds over the Sundays estate, the Forby road and the barren brown plain of the park. Silk's little herd of Friesians had returned to their pasture. They stood in a huddle under the cedars, bewildered by the smoke.

The Pathway was shaped like an arm with bent elbow, its shoulder the junction with the Forby road, its wrist and hand

—or perhaps its one pointing finger—a footpath which ran through hilly meadows and copses to Stowerton. Three houses and two bungalows had been built along this arm, but in its crook there were only open fields. The bungalows were identical, rather large pink plastered bungalows with red tiled roofs and detached garages. They stood 'in their gardens', as estate agents put it, meaning that there are sections of garden at the sides as well as at front and back. Some twenty feet separated one from the other, and a further twenty feet down stood a two-storey house. Similar building materials had been used for this house and the two dwellings on the upper arm, red brick, white stone, cedarwood, but they varied in size and in design. All had sparse lawns and flower-beds planted with unhappy-looking annuals.

'The Peverils came in first,' said Burden. 'Their place was finished in January. Miss Mowler and Dunsand both moved in in March. He came from Myringham, Miss Mowler from the town here and the Peverils from Brighton. The Robinsons retired here from London, moving in in April, and the Streets came here from up north last month.'

'Do they all have garden gates opening on to that bit of land between them and the quarry?' asked Wexford.

'Only the Peverils and the two bungalows. There was going to be a path made at the back, but someone got the planning authority to veto that.'

'We'll go and have a word with your Mrs Peveril.'

She was a very nervous woman, breathless with nerves. Wexford thought she was in her late thirties. Her hair-style and her clothes were fussy but not in any of the current modes. She dressed evidently in a somewhat modified version of the style of her youth, full, longish skirt, stilt heels. He sized her up immediately as belonging to a distinct and not uncommon type, the sheltered and conservative woman who, childless and exclusively dependent on her husband for all emotional needs, tends to be suspicious of other men and of the outside world.

Such women will go to almost any lengths to preserve their security and their absolute domestic quietude, so Wexford was rather surprised that Mrs Peveril had volunteered any information about a murder victim.

'All that smoke,' she said querulously, leading them into an over-neat living room. 'Isn't it dreadful? I shan't be able to get my washing out for hours. It was bad enough having that ghastly racket over the weekend—I didn't get a wink of sleep. The noise was frightful. I'm not surprised someone got murdered.'

'The murder,' said Wexford, 'happened several days before the festival started.'

'Did it?' Mrs Peveril looked unconvinced. 'When I heard someone had been killed I said to my husband, they took too many of those drugs they all take and someone went too far. D'you mind not sitting on that cushion? I've just put a fresh cover on it.'

Wexford moved on to a leather-seated and apparently invulnerable chair. 'I believe you saw the girl?'

'Oh, yes, I saw her. There's no doubt about that.' She gave a short nervous laugh. 'I don't know many people round here except my friend on the other side of the estate, but I knew that girl wasn't local. The people round here don't dress like that.'

'What made you notice her?'

'If you're going to ask me a lot of questions I'd like my husband to be present. I'll just call him. He's working but he won't mind stopping for a bit. I might say—well, the wrong thing if he wasn't here. I'll just call him.'

Wexford shrugged. In a manner of speaking, the 'wrong' thing could easily be the thing he wanted her to say. But she had asked for her husband as some people ask for their lawyers and probably with less need. He saw no reason to refuse his permission and he got up, smiling pleasantly, when Peveril came in.

'You didn't see the girl yourself, Mr Peveril?'

'No, I was working.' Peveril was one of those men who talk about work and working as if labour belongs exclusively to them, as if it is an arduous, exacting cross they must bear, while the rest of the world make carefree holiday. 'I work a ten-hour day. Have to what with the cost of running this place. The first I heard of any girl was when my wife told me last night she'd given information to the police.' He glared at Burden. 'I was working when you lot came.'

'Perhaps we shouldn't keep you from your work now?'

'Oh, please don't go, Edward, please don't. You said I was silly to say what I said last night and now . . .'

'I can do with a short break,' said Peveril lugubriously. 'I've been at it since eight, thanks to being made totally idle by a weekend of uproar. I'm worn out.'

Comforted but still jumpy, his wife rushed into the middle of things. 'It's a matter of chance I was here at all. I nearly went to the pictures—my husband had seen the film in London and told me to go—but it was such a lovely afternoon. I just looked out of the window there and I saw her. I saw this girl walking up towards the footpath.'

'Describe her to me. In as much detail as you can, please.'

'She was about my height and she had a lot of dyed blonde hair cut in the shaggy way they all go in for.' Mrs Peveril twitched at her own over-permed, frizzy dark hair with an unsteady hand. 'And she was very heavily made-up, tarty. She had on this trouser suit, bright mauve—it hurt your eyes —with a darker mauve edging to it, and mauve patent shoes with high heels. Her handbag was mauve, a great big showy handbag with a gilt buckle, and she was carrying a brown carrier bag. I watched her because I wanted to tell my husband what a sight she was—he's very particular in his tastes, being a sort of artist—and I save up little things to tell him when he's finished work.'

'But you didn't tell him, Mrs Peveril?'

'I must have forgotten.' She was suddenly flurried. 'I wonder why I didn't tell you, Edward?'

The 'sort of artist' turned down the corners of his mouth. 'I expect I was too tired to listen. If you've finished with her I'll get back to the grindstone.'

'I've almost finished. Where did she go?'

'Across the field,' said Mrs Peveril promptly. 'That is, down the footpath, you know. I stayed at the window a long time but she didn't come back.'

She came to the door with them and watched them nervously as they got back into their car. Wexford's driver, glancing up innocently, received from her such a sharp look that he went red and turned away.

'Well, Mike, I don't quite know what to make of the Peverils, but she certainly saw the girl. Her description was too accurate to admit of anything else. Our best bet is to conclude that Dawn went across that field to meet a man. Where would she have met him?'

'In the open, I suppose. If she was going to meet him in Stowerton she'd have gone to Stowerton—the buses go every ten minutes between four and seven. There's no shelter between here and Stowerton except trees and the old pumping station.'

Wexford nodded. He knew the place Burden spoke of, a shed containing disused pumping equipment and standing in thick woodland on the banks of the Kingsbrook.

'We'll have it searched,' he said. 'That's quite an idea. Meanwhile, I'd like to see how things are progressing in the High Street.'

Things had progressed considerably. When Wexford entered the hall of the Baptist church, Martin had two people waiting to see him, each with information that was to complicate rather than simplify the case.

The first of these, an assistant from the Snowdrop Laundry

and Dry Cleaners in Kingsmarkham High Street, was a middle-aged cheerful woman who had known Dawn Stonor as a schoolgirl and since then had sometimes seen her on her rare visits to her mother.

'We sort of knew each other by sight really,' she said. 'She came in last Monday at about a quarter past four.'

'She was dressed in mauve?'

'That's right. A very smart trouser suit. I remember we cleaned it for her Easter time. When she came in on Monday I wasn't sure if she knew me, but I asked her how her mum was and her gran and she said all right. Well, she'd brought this blue frock in to be cleaned and she wanted to know if I could get it done express. She wanted to collect it the next morning. "We can just do it," I said, "seeing you've brought it before four-thirty." If they come in later than that, you see, they can't get their things back before the next afternoon.

' "I want to be on the ten-fifteen train tomorrow," she said, "so can I collect it at ten?" '

'She meant to collect it herself?' Wexford asked.

'Well, she said "I". She didn't say anything about her mum fetching it like she has in the past. No, she meant to get it herself. I said that'd be all right and I made out the slip for her. You can see our part of it if you like. I've got it here with me.'

Wexford thanked her and examined the slip, noting the name and the date.

'But she didn't collect it?'

'No. I had it all ready but she never came. I was going to pop up to her mum's with it this week and then I heard what had happened. Awful, isn't it? It made me go cold all over when I heard.'

Next Wexford saw the manager of the Luximart, a big new supermarket which stood between the Dragon and the Baptist church just beside the Forby bus stop. He was young, eager and helpful.

'The young lady came in here at half past four. We don't

get many customers late on a Monday on account of we don't sell meat on a Monday and the veg isn't fresh. Most people eat up the Sunday leftovers and shop on Tuesdays.

'She was almost my last customer and when she left she waited nearly half an hour for the Forby bus, the five-twelve. Stood outside here, she did. I cursed, I can tell you, because just after the bus had come and she'd got on it I was sweeping up in the shop and I found this slip from the cleaners.'

'May I see?'

'I was certain she'd dropped it. I was sure it hadn't been there before she came in and I was quite worried thinking maybe she'd have trouble collecting her cleaning. I reckoned she'd come back but she never did. Then when I saw your notices and heard the name . . .'

'You didn't know her?'

'Never saw her before,' said the manager, 'that I can recall.'

Wexford matched the two slips, the top and the carbon. *Miss Stonor*, he read, *15 Lower Road, Kingsmarkham. Blue dress, express, 46p.* 'Will you describe her, please?'

'Nice-looking blonde. Very smartly dressed in a sort of purple blouse and slacks. I don't know, I can't describe girls' clothes. I reckon she had a purple bag. I remember thinking . . .' The manager looked up ruefully and bit his lip. 'I remember thinking she was a smashing piece, but it seems awful saying that now she's dead.'

'What did she buy?'

'I knew you'd ask me that. I've been trying to think. I was at the check-out and she called me over to the deep freeze and asked me what the strawberry sundaes were like. They're sort of mousse things in cartons. I said I'd recommend them and she put two in the trolley. Wait, I'm trying to see it, sort of get a picture . . .'

Wexford nodded, saying nothing. He knew that this method, a kind of free association, was the best way. Let the man close his eyes, transport himself mentally back into the shop, stand beside the girl, re-create the almost empty wire trolley . . .

'There was a can in the trolley.' He concentrated. 'I know what it was! Soup. Vichyssoise, the stuff you can have hot or cold. It's all coming back. She took a tin of chicken fillets off the shelf and tomatoes—yes, tomatoes in a pack. I think she bought bread, a cut loaf. She might have bought butter, I don't remember. I do remember she got a bottle of wine, though, because she had the cheapest line we do. Spanish beaujolais and some cigarettes. She hadn't a basket. I gave her a brown paper carrier.'

There was no one else to see. Wexford went back to the police station where he found Burden with the doctor. The wind rattled the windows and a thin rain spattered against the glass.

'She meant to spend the night here,' he said. 'She was going to call for that dress on Tuesday morning. And it was food she was carrying in that bag when Mrs Peveril saw her. Food for *two* people.'

'For her and her date,' said Burden.

'Then he wasn't a casual pick-up. A man she picked up would either not ask her to eat with him at all or else he'd invite her to some restaurant. You can't imagine a girl making a date with a stranger and that stranger saying, Bring a three-course meal with you and we'll have a picnic. She must have known him and known him well.' Wexford listed the items of food and said, 'What's the most interesting thing about that food, Mike?'

'It could have been eaten cold as it was or it could have been heated. In other words, it could have been bought especially to be eaten in the open air, or it could equally well have been heated—the soup and the chicken, that is—which means indoors, in a house.'

During this interchange the doctor, who had been sketching a duodenum on the back of Wexford's draft of the crime-prevention plans, looked up and said, 'It wasn't eaten at all.

I've got a provisional medical report prepared for you—there'll be a more detailed one later from the experts, of course—but the girl's stomach was empty. She hadn't eaten anything for five or six hours. Maybe the boy friend ate the lot on his own.'

'Or else food and wine and carrier bag are hidden somewhere with the mauve trouser suit.'

'Not the wine,' said Crocker. He stopped drawing and his face was suddenly grim. 'The wine was used. Remember the glass you found, Reg, the glass you cut your hand on? There was glass embedded in her face and neck. Her dress was stained with wine as well as blood. I don't think I'm being unduly melodramatic when I say that her attacker went completely mad. Perhaps you and Mike will be able to find out whatever it was she said or did to him. All I can say is that something she did tipped him over the edge. He beat her to death with that wine bottle. He beat her in such a frenzy that the glass broke against the bones of her face.'

It was dark inside the little shed, half-filled as it was by cumbersome, rusty machinery, and the men worked by the light of lamps they had brought with them. Outside the pumping station the river rattled noisily and the wind slapped the door monotonously against its rotted frame.

'If they came in here,' said Wexford at last, 'it was a very brief visit. No blood, no crumbs, no cigarette ends.' He touched his hair and brought away a handful of cobwebs. 'It's a filthy hole, not at all my idea of the sort of rendezvous likely to entice a girl like Dawn Stonor, who, I take it, was conscious of her appearance.' For a moment he watched the men lifting up old sacks and searching through coils of rotted rope. 'I wish to God I could understand why she put that red dress on,' he said. 'I've a feeling that if I could I'd have the key to the whole business.'

'Because she got dirty in here?' hazarded Burden.

'Doing what? Not eating, not smoking, not making love. Talking, maybe? Then where did the dress come from? She wasn't carrying it with her. Perhaps he was. I just don't think it's possible that in one day she got two garments soiled so as to be unwearable. The coincidence is too great, and it's beyond the bounds of credibility that he happened to have a dress with him ready for her to put on in case hers got dirty. And who was he?'

'We may get some help as far as that goes from the London end.'

'Let's hope so. Shall we go? All this dust is making me cough.'

What Burden termed help from the London end had come in while they were down by the river. It was not information, data, reported interviews, but help in actual human form. She was an attractive young woman, this girl who had shared a flat in Philimede Gardens, Earls Court, with Dawn Stonor. Wexford went into the interview room where they told him she was and found her drinking tea and chain-smoking, the ashtray on the table in front of her already choked with butts.

7

'My name's Joan Miall,' she said, shaking hands in a very forthright manner. 'An inspector came this morning and asked me a lot of questions. He said you'd want to see me and I thought I'd save you the trouble by coming to see you.' She was dark with a very pretty intelligent face and deep blue eyes. She looked about twenty-four. 'I still can't believe Dawn's dead. It seems so fantastic.'

'It's good of you to come, Miss Miall. I shall have a great deal to ask you so I think we'll go upstairs to my office where we can be more comfortable.'

In the lift she didn't speak but she lit another cigarette. Wexford understood that this heavy smoking was an antidote to shock. He approved her plain knee-length skirt and scarlet shirt, the healthy fine-boned face which, scarcely touched with make-up, was framed in shining hair, long and parted in the centre. Her hands were ringless, the nails short and lacquered pale pink. The pleasant, semi-living room appointments of his office seemed to set her more at ease. She relaxed, smiled and stubbed out her cigarette. 'I smoke too much.'

'Maybe,' he said. 'You were very fond of Dawn?'

She hesitated. 'I don't know really. I shared a flat with her for four years. We saw each other every day. We worked together. It was a shock.'

'You both worked at the Townsman Club?'

'Yes, that was where we met. We'd both been through a bit of a bad time. Dawn had been living with a man who was

58

almost pathologically jealous and I'd been sharing with my sister. My sister was terribly possessive. Dawn and I decided to take a flat together and we made a pact not to fuss each other and not to worry if the other one didn't always come home. That's why I wasn't worried. Not until Saturday. Then, I...'

'You're running on a bit, Miss Miall,' Wexford interrupted her. 'Tell me about last Monday first.'

The slight strain this called for demanded a fresh cigarette. She lit one, inhaled and leant back in her chair. 'Dawn had started a week's holiday the Saturday before, Saturday, June fourth. She couldn't make up her mind whether to go away or not. Her boy friend—he's called Paul Wickford and he keeps a garage near us—he wanted her to go touring in Devon with him, but she still hadn't decided by that Monday morning.'

'You expected her back on Monday evening?'

'Yes, in a way. She went off in the morning to catch the train for Kingsmarkham and she wasn't very cheerful. She never was when she was going to see her mother, they didn't get on. Dawn got on better with her grandmother.' Joan Miall paused and seemed to consider. 'Paul came round at about six, but when she hadn't come by seven he drove me to the club and then he went back to our flat to wait for her. Well, when she wasn't there on the Tuesday or the Wednesday and I didn't see anything of Paul, I thought they'd gone off to Devon together. We never left notes for each other, you see. We had this non-interference pact.'

'She told her mother she was working that night.'

Joan smiled slightly. 'I expect she did. That would just be an excuse to get away. Four or five hours in her mother's company would be as much as she could stand.' She stubbed out her cigarette, flicking ash fastidiously from her fingers. 'On Saturday—last Saturday, I mean—Paul appeared again. He hadn't been in Devon. His mother died that very Monday night and he'd had to go up north to the funeral and to see about things. He didn't know where Dawn was any more than I did.

'Then yesterday when we were both getting really worried—Dawn was due back at work tonight—the police came and told me what had happened.'

'Miss Miall, when Dawn was found she was wearing a dark red dress.' He noted her quick glance of surprise but ignored it for the moment. 'Now we have that dress here,' he said. 'It's rather badly stained. I'm going to ask you if you will be very brave and look at that dress. I warn you that you could find it upsetting. Will you look at it?'

She nodded.

'Yes, if you think it'll help. I can't remember Dawn ever wearing red. It wasn't her colour. But I'll look at it.'

The dress was made of a dark red rayon fabric with cap sleeves, a shaped waist and self belt. Because of its colour, the stains didn't show up except as a great stiff patch on the bodice.

The girl whitened and compressed her lips. 'May I touch it?' she said faintly.

'Yes.'

Rather tremulously, she fingered the neck opening and looked at the label. 'This is only a size twelve,' she said. 'Dawn was quite a big girl. She took a fourteen.'

'But she was wearing this dress.'

'It wasn't hers and it must have been quite a tight fit on her.' Abruptly she turned away and shivered. 'Look, perhaps you don't know much about fashion, but that dress is old, seven or eight years out of date, maybe more. Dawn was very fashion-conscious.'

Wexford led her back to his office. She sat down and the colour returned to her cheeks. He waited a little, marvelling at the friend's distress, the mother's indifference, and then he said, 'Miss Miall, will you try to give me a sort of character sketch of Dawn? What sort of girl she was, whom she knew and how she reacted to other people?'

'I'll try,' said Joan Miall.

'I don't want to give you the impression,' the girl began, 'that she wasn't a nice person. She was. But there were some—well, rather peculiar things about her.' She lifted her head and looked at him earnestly, almost aggressively.

'I'm not asking for a character *reference*, you know. And what you say will be between us. I shan't broadcast it about.'

'No, of course not. But she's dead and I have sort of old-fashioned ideas about not speaking ill of the dead. I expect you'll think that a doll who serves drinks in a club hasn't any right to get all upstage, sort of disapprove of other people's behaviour?'

Wexford didn't answer. He smiled gently and shook his head.

'Anyway,' she said, 'I didn't exactly disapprove of Dawn. It was just that—well, it's not always easy living with a compulsive liar. You don't know where you are with people like that. You don't know *them* and the relationship is sort of unreal. I know someone said that even a really bad liar tells more truth than lies, but you still can't tell what are lies and what truth, can you?'

It was on the tip of Wexford's tongue to ask what an intelligent girl like Joan Miall was doing at the Townsman Club, but he checked the impulse.

'So Dawn was a liar?' he said instead, reflecting that this wasn't going to make his task easier. He looked into the frank, clear eyes of the girl opposite him, a girl he was sure would be transparently truthful. 'What did she lie about?'

'Well, it was boasting and name-dropping really. She'd had an awful childhood. Her father used to knock her about, and her mother sort of knocked her about mentally. She'd tell her she was immoral and no good in one breath and then in the next she'd say how she missed her and begged her to come home and marry and settle down. Mrs Stonor was always telling her they were—what was the phrase?—Oh, yes, "Just ordinary folk", and Dawn had no business giving herself airs. Then she'd say the work she did was no better than being a tart.

'It made her want to prove herself. Sorry if I'm talking like an amateur psychiatrist but I'm interested in that sort of thing. I tried to find out what made Dawn tick. When we first lived together I thought she really did know a lot of famous people. One day she brought a dog home and said she was going to look after it for a fortnight while its owner was away. She said the owner was a famous actor, a household word more or less. He's always on television.

'Then, after the dog had gone back, we were both in the club one night and this actor came in. Some member brought him as his guest. Of course I recognised him. He didn't even know Dawn. It wasn't that they'd quarrelled and weren't speaking. You could tell he just didn't know her.' Joan shrugged. She put her cigarettes into her bag and closed the bag decisively. 'She used to look through the evening paper and she'd spot a photograph of some well-known guy and say she'd worked with him or had an affair with him. I never said much. It embarrassed me. The biggest name she ever dropped was a singer, terribly famous. She said she'd known him for years and every so often they'd go out together. She *said*. A couple of weeks ago the phone rang and she answered it. She looked at me and covered up the mouthpiece and said it was him, but when she started talking to him she never said his name, just "Yes" and "No" and "That'd be lovely". She never actually called him Zeno. You can pretend a phone-caller is anyone, can't you? Your flatmate's not likely to go and listen on the extension.'

'Zeno?' said Wexford. 'D'you mean she claimed acquaintance with Zeno Vedast?'

'That's rather the word, "claimed". He never came to the flat. I never saw her with him. No, it was just the same as with the TV actor, name-dropping to impress, I'm afraid.'

'Miss Miall, was Dawn the sort of girl who might pick up a stranger and spend the night with him?'

She hesitated and then said impulsively, 'She might have. It sounds hateful but Dawn was very fond of money. She never had any money when she was a child, just a shilling a week or something ridiculous, and she was supposed to save half of that in a piggy bank you couldn't open. And her parents can't have been that poor—they both worked. I'm telling you this to explain why she might have picked someone up if she thought there was anything in it for her. When she first came to the club she was told like we all are that dating a customer means instant dismissal. The members know that but some of them try it on. Well, Dawn accepted an invitation from a member, in spite of the rule. He said if she'd go away for the weekend with him he'd buy her a fur coat. She did go and he gave her ten pounds. She never got the coat and I think she felt awfully humiliated because she never did that again. She liked admiration too and if a man wanted to sleep with her she thought . . . Oh, well, that it means a lot more than it does. Sometimes when she wasn't working she'd be away for a night and I think she was with a man. She couldn't bring him home, you see, in case Paul came round. But, as I told you, we didn't ask each other questions.'

'This Mr Wickford was a steady boy friend?'

She nodded. 'They'd been going out together for two years. I think she'd have married Paul in the end. The trouble seemed to be that he wasn't rich enough for her or famous or anything. He's about thirty-five, divorced, very nice. He was frightfully upset when he heard what had happened to her and the doctor had to give him sedatives. I'm sure she would have married him if she could only have grown out of all those ideas about knowing famous people. She was a very nice girl really, generous, good fun, always ready to help anyone out. It was just that she couldn't help telling lies...'

'One last thing. Miss Miall. Dawn brought food in Kingsmarkham last Monday afternoon, a tin of soup, tinned chicken and two strawberry mousse things in cartons. Is it possible she bought it to take home for lunch for the two of you on Tuesday?'

'Definitely not.'

'Why are you so sure?'

'For one thing—please don't think I don't like this place, it's a very nice town—but no one who lives—er, lived—where Dawn did would buy food here to take home. We're surrounded by delicatessen shops and big supermarkets. The other thing is, she wouldn't buy food for the two of us. I'm a bit of a faddist when it comes to food. Health-conscious. You wouldn't think so the way I smoke, would you?' She gave a slight laugh. 'I never eat food out of cans. Dawn knew that. We used to prepare our food quite separately unless one of us made a casserole or a salad. Dawn didn't care what she ate. She hated cooking and she used to say she ate to live.' Joan winced at the last word which had been used automatically, without thought. She lifted her eyes to Wexford and he saw that they shone with unshed tears. In a choking voice she said:

'She didn't live very long, did she?'

Michael Burden was a widower whose married life had been happy and who, as a result of this, tended to consider sexual relationships as ecstatically romantic or, when they were illicit, deeply sordid. But the solitary love affair he had had since his wife's death had slightly broadened his mind. He was now prepared to admit that unmarried people might love each other and consummate that love without degradation. Sometimes these newly enlightened views of his gave rise to romantic theories and it was one of these which he propounded to

Wexford as they drank their coffee together on Tuesday morning.

'We've agreed,' he began, 'that her killer can't have been a casual pick-up because of the food-shopping angle. And we know the food wasn't bought for her and the Miall girl. Therefore, she knew the man and knew him well enough to arrange with him that she'd buy their meal and meet him after he'd finished work. The time of the meeting—surely between five-thirty and six?—indicates it was to be after he'd finished work. Right?'

'Imagine so, Mike.'

'Well, sir, I've been wondering if she and this bloke had one of those long close friendships extending over years.'

'What long close friendships? What are you on about?'

'You know my sister-in-law Grace?' Wexford nodded impatiently. Of course he knew Grace, the sister of Burden's dead wife who had looked after Burden's children when they had first lost their mother and who he had later hoped would be the second Mrs Burden. That had come to nothing. Grace had married someone else and now had a baby of her own. 'I mention her,' said Burden, 'because it was her experience that gave me the idea. She and Terry knew each other off and on for years before they got married. There was always a sort of bond between them, although they didn't meet much and each of them had other—well, friends. Terry even got engaged to someone else.'

'You're suggesting this was the case with Dawn?'

'She lived here till she was eighteen. Suppose she knew this bloke when they were both very young and they had an affair and then they both left Kingsmarkham to work elsewhere. Or he stayed here and she went to London. What I'm suggesting is that they kept in touch and whenever she came home or he went to London they had one of these dates, secret dates necessarily because he was married and she was more or less engaged to Wickford. Frankly, I think this covers every

65

aspect of the case and deals with all the difficulties.'

Wexford stirred his coffee, looked longingly towards the sugar bowl and resisted the temptation to take another lump. 'It doesn't deal with that bloody red dress,' he said viciously.

'It does if they met in this chap's house. We'd have to admit the possibility of coincidence, that she stained the mauve outfit and then put on a dress belonging to this man's wife.'

'The wife being out presumably. She goes there, he lets her in. What happens to the mauve garment? They had no drinks for her to spill, ate nothing for her to drop, made no love to —er, crush it. (I put it like that, Mike, to save your delicate sensibilities.) Maybe the violence of his welcoming embrace creased it up and she was so dainty about her appearance that she rushed upstairs and slipped into one of her rival's ancient cast-offs. He was so upset about her thinking more of her clothes than of him that he upped and banged her with the bottle. Is that it?'

'It must have been something like that,' said Burden rather stiffly. Wexford was always pouring cold water on his flights of fancy and he never got used to it.

'Where was this house of assignation, then?'

'On the outskirts of Stowerton, the Forby side. She went by the fields because he was going to meet her there and take her back to his house. They arranged it that way just in case the wife changed her mind about going away.' He made a moue of distaste, sordidness temporarily conquering romance. 'Some people do go on like that, you know.'

'You seem to know, anyway. So all we have to do now is find a bloke living in a house on the north side of Stowerton who's known Dawn Stonor since they went to Sunday school together and whose wife was away Monday night. Oh, and find if the wife has missed a red dress.'

'You don't sound too enthusiastic, sir.'

'I'm not,' Wexford said frankly. 'The people you know may go on like that but the people I know don't. They act like *people*, not characters in a second feature film that's been thrown together for the sake of sensation rather than illustrating human nature. But since my mind is otherwise a blank, I reckon we'd better get asking Mrs Stonor who Dawn knew around Stowerton and who had a lifelong sentimental bond with her.'

8

'The folks round here,' said Mrs Stonor, 'weren't good enough for Dawn. She was a proper little snob, though what she'd got to be snobbish about I never will know.'

For all her frankly expressed unmaternal sentiments, Mrs Stonor was dressed in deepest black. She and the old woman who was with her, and who had been introduced as 'My mother, Mrs Peckham', had been sitting in semi-darkness, for the curtains were drawn. When the two policemen entered the room a light was switched on. Wexford noticed that a wall mirror had been covered by a black cloth.

'We think it possible,' he said, 'that Dawn went to meet an old friend on Monday night. I want you to try and remember the names of any boy friends she had before she left home or any name she may have mentioned to you on her visits here.'

Instead of replying, Mrs Stonor addressed the old woman who was leaning forward avidly, clutching the two sticks that supported her when she walked. 'You can get off back to bed now, Mother. All this has got nothing to do with you. You've been up too long as it is.'

'I'm not tired,' said Mrs Peckham. She was very old, well over eighty. Her body was thin and tiny and her face simian, a maze of wrinkles. What sparse white hair she had was scragged on to the top of her head into a knot stuck full of pins. 'I don't want to go to bed, Phyllis. It's not often I have a bit of excitement.'

'Excitement! I like that. A nice way to talk when Dawn's

had her head bashed in by a maniac. Come along now. I'll take your arm up the stairs.'

A small devil in Wexford's head spoke for him. 'Mrs Peckham should stay. She may be able to help.' He said it more to irritate Mrs Stonor than because he thought her mother would be able to furnish them with information.

Mrs Peckham grinned with pleasure, showing a set of over-large false teeth. Reprieved, she helped herself to a sweet from the bag on a table beside her and began a ferocious crunching. Her daughter turned down the corners of her mouth and folded her hands.

'Can you think of anyone, Mrs Stonor?'

Still sulky from having her wishes baulked, Mrs Stonor said, 'Her dad never let her have boy friends. He wanted her to grow up respectable. We had a job with her as it was, always telling lies and staying out late. My husband tried every way we could think of to teach her the meaning of decency.'

'Tried his strap, mostly,' said Mrs Peckham. Protected by the presence of the policemen, she gave her daughter a triumphant and unpleasant grin. Wexford could see that she was one of those old pensioners who, dependent for all her needs on a hated child, was subservient, cringing, defiant or malicious as her fancy took her or circumstances demanded. When Mrs Stonor made no reply but only lifted her chin, her mother tried another dig. 'You and George ought never to have had no kids. Always smacking her and yelling at her. Knock one devil out and two in, that's what I say.'

Wexford cleared his throat. 'We don't seem to be getting very far. I can't believe Dawn never mentioned any man she was friendly with.'

'I never said she didn't. You'll get your stomach trouble again, Mother, if you don't leave them acid drops alone. The fact is, it was all lies with Dawn. I got so I let what she said go in one ear and out the other. I do know she had this man

Wickford on account of her bringing him down here for the day last year. They didn't stop long. Dawn could see what I thought about *him*. A divorced man, running a garage! That was the best she could do for herself.'

'There was no one else?' Burden asked coldly.

'I said I *don't know*. You're not going to tell me she got herself done in by some boy she was at school with, are you? That's all the local boys she knew.'

Mrs Peckham, having incompletely unwrapped her latest sweet, was removing shreds of paper from her mouth. 'There was Harold Goodbody,' she said.

'Don't be so stupid, Mother. As if Harold'd have anything to do with a girl like Dawn. Harold climbed too high for the likes of her.'

'Who is this man?' asked Wexford.

The sweet lodged in a wizened cheek pouch, the noisy sucking abated, Mrs Peckham heaved a heavy but not unhappy sigh. 'He was a lovely boy, was Harold. Him and his mum and dad used to live round here in the next street. I wasn't here then, I had my own cottage, but I used to see Harold when I had my job serving dinners at the school. Oh, he was a lad! Always one for a joke was Harold, April Fools all the year round for him. Him and Dawnie was pals from their first day at school. Then I come here to live with Phyllis and George and Dawnie'd bring him back to tea.'

'I never knew that,' said Mrs Stonor, bristling. 'George wouldn't have had that.'

'George wasn't here, was he? And you was working at that shop. I didn't see no harm in Dawnie bringing her friend home.' Mrs Peckham turned her back on her daughter and faced Wexford. 'Harold was a real freak to look at, all bones and his hair nearly as white as mine. I'd have boiled eggs all ready for the three of us, but when Dawnie and me started cracking ours we'd find just the empty shells. Harold'd brought a couple of empty shells to fool us. Ooh, he was

70

funny! He had a joke ink blot and a rubber spider. Made us scream, that spider did. One day I caught him playing with the phone. He'd rung this number and when the woman answered he said he was the engineers. He said to her there was an emergency. She was to pour boiling water down the receiver, leave it for ten minutes and then cut the lead with scissors. She was going to too, she believed him, but I put a stop to that, though I was laughing fit to die. Harold was a real scream.'

'Yes, I'm sure,' said Wexford. 'How old was he when all this fun and games was going on?'

'About fifteen.'

'And he still lives round here?'

'No, of course he don't. That Mr Silk from Sundays took him up and he left home and went to London when he was seventeen and got famous, didn't he?'

Wexford blinked. 'Famous? Harold Goodbody?'

Mrs Peckham wagged her gnarled hands impatiently. 'He changed his name when he got to be a singer. What did he call himself? Now I'm getting on I seem to forget everything. John Lennon, that was it.'

'I hardly think . . .' Wexford began.

Mrs Stonor, who had remained silent and scornful, opened her mouth and snapped, 'Zeno Vedast. He calls himself Zeno Vedast.'

'Dawn was at school with Zeno Vedast?' Wexford said blankly. So it hadn't been all boasting, vain name-dropping? Or some of it hadn't. 'They were friends?'

'You don't want to listen to Mother,' said Mrs Stonor. 'I daresay Dawn saw a bit of him when they were at school. She never saw him in London.'

'Oh, yes, she did, Phyllis. She told me so last Monday when she was home. She'd tell me things she'd never tell you. She knew you'd pour cold water on everything she did.'

71

'What did she say, Mrs Peckham?'

'She come into my room when I was in bed. You remember Hal, don't you, Gran? she says. We always called him Hal. Well, I went out to dinner with him Friday night, she said.'

'And you believed her?' Mrs Stonor gave the brittle laugh that is not a laugh at all. 'Harold Goodbody was in Manchester Friday night. I saw him myself on telly, I saw him live. She was just making up tales like she always did.'

Mrs Peckham scrunched indignantly. 'She got the night wrong, that's all. Poor little Dawnie.'

'Don't you be so stupid. He's a *famous* singer. Though what's so wonderful about his voice I never shall know. Richard Tauber, now that was a man who *had* a voice.'

Burden asked, 'Do his parents still live here?'

Mrs Stonor looked for a moment as if she was going to tell him not to be so stupid. She restrained herself and said sourly, 'When he got rich he bought them a great big detached place up near London. All right for some, isn't it? I've always been decent and brought my daughter up right and what did she ever do for me? I well remember Freda Goodbody going round to her neighbours to borrow a quarter of tea on account of Goodbody spending all his wages on the dogs. Harold never had more than one pair of shoes at a time and they was cast-offs from his cousin. "My darling boy" and "my precious Hal" she used to say but she used to give him baked beans for his Sunday dinner.'

Suddenly Mrs Peckham waxed appropriately biblical. ' "Better a dish of herbs where love is",' she said, ' "than a stalled ox and hatred therewith".' She took the last acid drop and sucked it noisily.

'There you are, sir,' said Burden when they were in the car. 'A lifelong friendship, like I said.'

'Well, not quite like you said, Mike. Zeno Vedast doesn't live in Stowerton, he has no wife, and I don't suppose he makes a habit of eating tinned food in fields with waitresses.

72

The odd thing is that she *did* know him. It seems to bear out what Joan Miall said that, in the nature of things, even a chronic liar must tell more truth than lies. We all know the story of the boy who cried wolf. Dawn Stonor was a lion-hunter. She cried lion and this time the lion was real. But we haven't a shred of evidence to connect Vedast with her last Monday. Very likely he was still in Manchester. All I can say at the moment is that it's intriguing, it's odd.'

'Surely you think we ought to see him?'

'Of course we must see him. We must see every man Dawn knew, unless he has a watertight alibi for that Monday night. We still don't know what Wickford was doing after seven.' The chief inspector tapped his driver's shoulder. 'Back to the station, please, Stephens.'

The man half-turned. He was young, rather shy, recently transferred from Brighton. He blushed when Wexford addressed him, rather as he had coloured under Mrs Peveril's stare.

'Did you want to say something to me?' Wexford asked gently.

'No, sir.'

'Back to the station, then. We can't sit here all day.'

By Wednesday Paul Wickford had been cleared of suspicion. After leaving Joan Miall at the Townsman Club in Hertford Street, he had gone into a pub in Shepherd Market where he had drunk one vodka and tonic before driving back to Earls Court. Waiting for him in his flat was his brother who brought the news of their mother's serious illness and asked Paul to drive with him immediately to Sheffield. Paul had then asked the tenant of the second floor flat to cancel his milk and papers and, if he happened to see Dawn Stonor, to tell her where he had gone. The two brothers had reached their mother's house in Sheffield soon after midnight, and by the following morning she was dead.

In spite of there being only thin evidence of Dawn's killer having lived on the outskirts of Stowerton, a house-to-house investigation had begun on Tuesday afternoon of the whole district. No one had seen Dawn; no one had seen a girl in mauve alone or with a man. Only two wives had been absent from home on the evening in question, one with her husband and one leaving him behind to mind their four children. No wife had been away for the whole night and no wife had missed a red dress. Wexford's men searched the fields for the trouser suit and the food. It was dreary work, for the rain fell heavily and there were fears that the river would flood.

Mrs Clarke and Mrs Peveril remained the only people who had seen Dawn after five-twenty, Mrs Peveril the last person —except her killer—to have seen her alive. Wexford concentrated on these two women, questioning them exhaustively, and it wasn't long before he found something odd in their evidence. It had not previously occurred to him that they might know each other, and it was only when, sitting in Mrs Clarke's living room, listening to her answer the phone, that the thought occurred to him.

'I can't talk now, Margaret. I'll ring you later. I hope Edward soon feels better.'

She didn't say who had been at the other end of the line. Why should she? She sat down with a bright, insincere smile. 'So sorry. You were saying?'

Wexford said sharply, 'Were you talking to Mrs Peveril?'

'How *could* you know? I was, as a matter of fact.'

'Then I imagine you are the one person she claims acquaintance with in this district?'

'Poor Margaret. She's so neurotic and she has an awful time with Edward. I suppose I am her only friend. She doesn't make friends easily.'

'Mrs Clarke, you were first questioned about Dawn Stonor last Sunday evening, I think? We questioned people on this side of the estate first.'

'Well, you ought to know that better than me.'

She looked a little offended, bored, but not at all frightened. Wexford considered carefully. Burden and Martin and Gates had begun their questions here at seven, not reaching The Pathway till nine. 'Did you phone Mrs Peveril on Sunday evening before nine?' Her glance became wary, defensive. 'I see you did. You told her you'd been questioned and, moreover, that you'd been able to help. It was only natural for you to talk to your friend about it. I expect you described the girl to her and told her which way you'd seen her go.'

'Is there anything wrong in that?'

'Discretion would have been wiser. Never mind. Describe Dawn Stonor to me again now, please.'

'But I've done it hundreds of times,' cried Mrs Clarke with exasperated exaggeration. 'I've told you over and over again.'

'Once more, for the last time.'

'I was coming along to get the bus into Kingsmarkham. I saw her get off the bus that went the other way. She crossed the road and went into The Pathway.' Mrs Clarke spoke slowly and deliberately as might a parent explaining for the dozenth time to a not very bright child the point of a simple story. 'She had fair hair, she was in her twenties, and she wore a lilac-coloured trouser suit and mauve shoes.'

'That was what you told Mrs Peveril?'

'Yes, and you and all your other people. I couldn't say any more because I don't know any more.'

'You didn't, for instance, notice her large mauve bag with a gilt buckle or that there was a darker edging to the suit?'

'No, I didn't. I didn't notice that and you saying it doesn't bring it back to me or anything. I'm sorry but I've told you everything I know.'

He shook his head, not in denial of her statement, but at his own bewilderment. At first, briefly, when she put the phone down he had suddenly been certain that Mrs Peveril had never seen Dawn at all, that the news from her friend had sparked off an urge for sensationalism, giving her an opportunity to make herself important. He remembered how, although she said she had taken careful note of the girl's appearance in order to tell her husband about her, she had never told him. But now he knew she must have seen her. How else could she, and she alone, have known of the bag and the purple border to the tunic?

9

Three houses that backed on to Sundays, three garden gates opening on to a narrow strip of land beyond which was the quarry. . . . Each garden separated from its neighbours by high woven chestnut fencing, a strip of land overgrown with dense bushes and quite tall trees. Wexford thought how easy it would have been to carry a body out of one of those houses by night and drop it into the quarry. And yet, if Dawn had gone into one of those houses instead of across the fields, if Mrs Peveril had seen her do so and was a seeker after sensation, wouldn't these facts have made a far greater sensation?

'I thought you'd leave me alone after I'd told you the truth,' said Mrs Peveril fretfully. 'I shall be ill if you badger me. All right, Mrs Clarke did phone me. That doesn't mean I didn't see her too, does it? I saw her and I saw her walk across those fields.'

'She couldn't have gone into any of those houses, anyway, sir,' said Burden. 'Unless it was into Mrs Peveril's own house. In which case Mrs P. presumably wouldn't say she'd seen her at all. Dawn can't have gone into Dunsand's or Miss Mowler's. We've checked at Myringham, at the university, and Dunsand didn't leave there till six. He'd have been lucky to get home by six-thirty, more like twenty to seven. Miss Mowler was with her friend in Kingsmarkham till a quarter to eight.'

They went back to the police station and were about to enter the lift when a sharp draught of wind told Wexford that the double doors to the entrance foyer had been swept un-ceremoniously open. He turned round and saw an extra-ordinary figure. The man was immensely tall—far taller than Wexford who topped six feet—with a bush of jet-black hair. He wore an ankle-length pony-skin coat and carried a canvas bag whose sopping wet contents had soaked the canvas and were dripping on to the floor. Once inside, he paused, looked about him confidently and was making for Sergeant Camb who sat drinking tea behind his counter when Wexford inter-cepted him.

'Mr Mbowele, I believe? We've met before.' Wexford put out his hand which was immediately gripped in a huge copper-coloured vice of bone-crushing fingers. 'What can I do for you?'

The young African was extremely handsome. He had all the glowing virile grace which has led clothes designers and model agencies and photographers to take up the slogan—'Black is beautiful'. Beaming at Wexford, his soft, dark eyes alight, he withdrew his hand, dropped the sodden bag on to the floor and undid the collar of his coat. Under it his chest was bare, hung with a chain of small green stones.

'I don't altogether dig this rain, man,' he said, shaking drops of water off his hair. 'You call this June?'

'I'm not responsible for the weather.' Wexford pointed to the bag. 'And rain wasn't responsible for that unless the floods have started.'

'I fished it out of the river,' said Louis Mbowele. 'Not here. At Myringham. That's quite a river now, your little Kings-brook, man. I go down the river every morning and walk. I can think down there.' He stretched out his arms. It was easy to imagine him striding by the full flowing river, his mind equally in spate, his body brimming with vibrant energy. 'I was thinking,' he said, 'about Wittgenstein's principle of atomicity....'

'About *what*?'

'For an essay. It's not important. I looked in the river and I saw this purple silk thing ...'

'Is that what's in the bag?'

'Didn't you get that? I knew what it was, man, I'd read the papers. I waded in and fished it out and put it in this bag—it's my girl friend's bag—and brought it here.'

'You shouldn't have touched it, Mr Mbowele.'

'Louis, man, Louis. We're all friends, aren't we? I've no prejudice against the fuzz. The fuzz have their place in a well-organised state. I'm no anarchist.'

Wexford sighed. 'You'd better come upstairs and bring the bag with you.'

In the office Louis made himself immediately at home by taking off the pony-skin coat and drying his hair on its lining. He sat on a chair like one who is more accustomed to sit on the floor, one long leg stuck out and the other hooked over the chair arm.

'Exactly where did you find this, Louis?'

'In the river between Mill Street and the college grounds. It'd been swept down from round here somewhere. Look, why freak out about it? If I'd left it there it'd be down by the sea somewhere now. Keep your cool, man.'

'I am not losing my cool,' said Wexford who couldn't help smiling. 'Was there anything else in the river?'

'Fish,' said Louis, grinning, 'and sticks and stones and a hell of a lot of water.'

It was pointless, anyway, to ask about the paper carrier of food. What carrier bag, what cardboard cartons, would survive ten days and fifteen miles of pounding in that swollen stream? The can and the jar would survive, of course. But only a miracle would have brought them to precisely the same spot in the river as the trouser suit when Louis Mbowele had found it. Maybe the Wittgenstein principle provided for that sort of coincidence, but Wexford decided not to pursue it. The bag and, to a lesser extent the coat, were soaking his carpet.

'Well, I'm very grateful to you. You've been most public-spirited.' Wexford risked his hand again and managed not to wince when the vice enclosed it. 'There's a bus goes to Myringham at ten past which you ought to be in time for.'

'I ought if I'm going to get to Len's tutorial.' He glanced at the window. It was pouring. 'Have you ever been to Marumi?'

'Marumi?'

'My country. Sometimes you get no rain there for three years. Man, is that country dry! You like the sun?'

'It makes a change,' said Wexford.

'You said I was to remember you when I came into my kingdom. It won't be a kingdom but I'll need fuzz and I could get along great with you if you got rid of your hang-ups. How does it grab you?'

'I'll be too old by that time, Louis.'

'Age,' said the philosopher, 'is just a state of mind.' He looked, Wexford thought, about twenty. 'It won't be that long, man, not long at all. Get yourself together. Think it over.'

From the window Wexford watched him cross the street, swinging the wet, empty bag. He chuckled. When Burden came into the room, he looked up from the mauve rags he was examining.

'Just been offered a job, Mike.'

'Doing what?'

'My own thing, man, my own thing. When the rain and boredom here freak me out I can go boss the fuzz in a sort of black Ruritania. Can you see me in epaulettes with a Mauser on each hip?'

'My God,' said Burden. He fingered the torn material fastidiously. 'Is that the missing suit?'

Wexford nodded. 'Down to the purple edging, as described by our accurate Mrs Peveril. Louis Mbowele found it in the river at Myringham. It had obviously been washed down there by the heavy rains.'

'From those fields?'

'From up there somewhere. She was killed up there. I'm as sure of that as I'm sure I'll never be the Maigret of Marumi.'

Wexford remembered Miss Mowler from when she had been a district nurse in Kingsmarkham. His wife had broken her ankle and Miss Mowler had called three times a week to bath her and keep an eye on the plaster cast. She greeted him like an old friend.

'Mrs Wexford not been climbing any more ladders, I hope? And how are your lovely girls? I saw Sheila on television last week. She's getting quite well known, isn't she? And amazingly good-looking.'

'You mean it's amazing with me for her dad?'

'Oh, Mr Wexford, you know I didn't mean that!' Miss Mowler blushed and looked very confused. She tried to cover her gaffe with a string of explanations, but Wexford laughed and cut her short.

'I've come to talk to you about this murder, Miss Mowler.'

'But I can't help you. I wasn't here.'

'No, but you were here later in the evening. If there was anything you noticed, any little oddity . . .'

'I really can't help you,' she said earnestly. 'I've only been here three months and I hardly even know my neighbours.'

'Tell me what you do know of them, of the Peverils especially.'

The hall of the bungalow was rather garishly decorated, black and gilt predominating. The black bitumastic flooring curved upwards at the edges to meet an astonishingly hideous wallpaper. Wexford was rather surprised that sprays of lipstick-red flowers, each petal a pear-shaped scarlet blot, with spiralling black stems and glossy golden leaves, should be to Miss Mowler's taste. He did not tell her so as she led him into the living room, but he must have looked it, for she plunged into characteristic excuses.

'Awful, isn't it? The builder finished both these bungalows

81

completely before he sold them. Dreadful taste. You see I've got blue birds and orange lilies on the walls in here. And Mr Dunsand's next door is exactly the same. I believe he's going to re-decorate completely in his holidays. But doing that is so expensive and arduous if you're a lone woman like I am. The trouble is it's very good-quality paper and completely washable. I don't know if the Peverils' is the same. I believe they were able to choose their own decorations, but I've never been in there.'

'Mrs Peveril is a strange woman.'

'A very neurotic one, I should think. I heard her quarrelling once in the garden with her husband. She was crying quite hysterically.'

'What were they quarrelling about, Miss Mowler?' Wexford asked.

'Well, she was accusing him of being unfaithful to her. I couldn't help overhearing.' Afraid of another digression in which a spate of excuses would be put forward, Wexford shook his head and smiled. 'Oh, well, it's different rather with a policeman, isn't it? It's not gossip. Mrs Peveril's talked to me in the street. I hardly know her but that doesn't stop her saying the most—well, intimate things. I do think it's a mistake for a man to work at home, don't you?'

'Why, Miss Mowler?'

'He and his wife never get away from each other. And if the wife's possessive and jealous she'll resent it and begin suspecting things if ever he does go out without her. Mrs Peveril seems to depend on her husband for every sort of support, and of course the poor man isn't adequate. Who is? I don't think he wanted to come here. She was the moving spirit behind that . . . Oh, I didn't mean to make a pun. She's the sort of woman who's always running away if you know what I mean.'

'Does she ever go out without her husband?'

'Oh dear, women like that can never appreciate that what's

sauce for the goose ought to be sauce for the gander. She certainly goes out to her dressmaking class every Monday evening and sometimes she has another evening out with Mrs Clarke.'

'I suppose you knew Dawn Stonor?'

Any allegation that she might have been acquainted with a murder victim might have been expected to evoke fulsome excuses from a woman of Miss Mowler's temperament. Instead, she set her mouth and looked affronted. 'Very selfish, flighty sort of girl. I know the family very well. Naturally, I look in on the grandmother, Mrs Peckham, from time to time. It would have made a world of difference to that old lady's life if Dawn had bothered to go home more often. But there you are, that's the young people of today all over. While I was still working I used to tell Dawn about it but she fired right up at me, said she couldn't stand the place or her mother. There was some nonsense about having had an unhappy childhood. They've all had unhappy childhoods, Mr Wexford, to account for every bit of bad behaviour.' She tossed her head. 'I haven't seen her for two or three years now and I can't say I'm sorry.'

It was such a change for Miss Mowler not to be able to say she was sorry that Wexford concluded Dawn's firing up must have riled her excessively. He thanked her and left. Dunsand's bungalow had the closed-up, discouraging look of a house that is seldom ocupied by day, all the windows shut, a milk bottle with a note stuck in it on the doorstep. He caught sight of Mrs Peveril, neatly overalled, watering a window box. She saw him, pretended she hadn't, and rushed indoors, slamming the front door.

She was a biggish woman, the victim of premature middle-aged spread, several stones heavier than Miss Mowler who was twenty-five years her senior. He hadn't really noticed that before. She wouldn't be a size twelve, more a sixteen. But a woman can put on a lot of weight in seven years, and Joan

83

Miall had said the dress was seven or eight years old . . .

He had himself driven to Lower Road and again he was aware of a fidgety unease on the part of young Stevens, his driver. These days the man seemed always on the point of saying something to him, of unburdening his soul perhaps. He would say 'Yes, sir' and 'No, sir', but there was no finality about these responses, rather a vague note of hesitation and often a preoccupied pause before the man turned away and started the car. Wexford tried asking him what was the matter but he was always answered by a respectful shake of the head, and he concluded that Stevens had some domestic trouble weighing on him that he longed to discuss but was too shy and too reticent to reveal.

Mrs Stonor was in her kitchen, ironing, her mother in a rocking chair beside her. It was a chair which squeaked each time it was moved and Mrs Peckham, who seemed in an even more maliciously cheerful frame of mind today, moved it constantly, taking delight in the noise it made—they say you cannot make a noise to annoy yourself—and munching Edinburgh rock.

'I never heard her mention no Peveril,' said Mrs Stonor, passing her iron across a pair of pink locknit knickers that could only have belonged to her mother yet were capacious enough to have contained the whole of that little, dried-up body. 'She was proud of *not* knowing anyone around here, called them provincials or some fine thing. There's ever such a nice woman as is manageress of the cleaners and she'd known Dawn all her life. Dawn had to pretend she'd never seen her before. What d'you think of that?'

Wexford had to keep his thoughts to himself. He was marvelling, not for the first time, at certain popular fallacies. That children naturally love their parents is a belief which has all but died away. The world still holds that parents love their children, love them automatically, through thick and thin, through disappointment and disillusion. He himself had until recently believed that the loss of a child is the one insupportable grief. When would people come to understand that the death of a son or daughter, removing the need of a parent to put a good face on things, to lie to neighbours, to sustain a false image, can be a relief?

'If she had fallen in love with a local man,' he said carefully, 'perhaps these prejudices of hers wouldn't have counted for much.' He knew as he spoke that he was talking a foreign language to Mrs Stonor.

She seized upon the one point that meant anything to her. 'She wasn't capable of loving anyone.'

Mrs Peckham snorted. With surprising psychological insight, she said, 'Maybe she didn't know how. Kids don't know how if they don't get none theirselves. Same thing with dogs.' She passed Wexford the bag of rock and grinned grimly when he took a piece. 'And monkeys,' she added. 'I read that in me *Reader's Digest*.'

'We're wondering, Mrs Stonor, if she went into a man's house.' With any other bereaved mother he would have softened his words; with this one any tact seemed a superfluous sentimentality. 'We think she may have had an assignation with a local man while his wife was away.'

'I wouldn't put it past her. She hadn't got no morals. But she wouldn't go to a fellow's house—even I can see that. That's stupid. She'd got a flat of her own, hadn't she? Them girls was only too ready to make themselves scarce if the other one was up to any funny business.' It was atrociously put, but it was unanswerable. 'Dawn didn't even have the decency to hide any of that from me,' Mrs Stonor said fiercely. 'She told me she'd been with men in that way. She called it being honest and leading her own life. As if she knew the meaning of honesty! I'd have died before I'd have told such things to my mother.'

A shrieking cackle came from Mrs Peckham. 'You'd nothing to tell, Phyllis. You aren't 'uman.'

'Don't be so stupid, Mother. The sergeant don't want you poking your nose in all the time, and it's time you had your rest. You've been fancying yourself ever since that young man come to see you this morning, buttering you up like I don't know what.'

Amused at his sudden demotion two rungs down the ladder, Wexford, who had risen to go, gave the older woman a conspiratorial half-smile. 'A grandson, Mrs Peckham?'

'No, I never had no kids but Phyllis. More's the pity.' She said it not as if she pined for a replica of Mrs Stonor but perhaps for her antithesis. 'Mind you, he was like a grandson in a way, was Hal.'

'Will you do as I ask, Mother, and get off to bed?'

'I'm going, Phyllis. I'm on me way.' An awareness that, after all, she depended for her bed and board on her daughter's good graces briefly softened Mrs Peckham's asperity, but not for long. She heaved herself up, clutching her sweets. 'You've got it in for poor Hal just because he wasn't all over you like he was me. He kissed me,' she said proudly.

'Mrs Peckham, am I right in thinking that Zeno Vedast has been here to see you? Do you mean while the festival was on? You didn't tell me that before.'

She propped herself on her walking aid, hunching her thin shoulders. 'He come this morning,' she said. 'Looking out for a house for hisself round here, one of them big places as we used to call gentlemen's houses. Ooh, he's very grand in his ideas, is Hal. He's got a whole suite to hisself at that big hotel in the Forest, but he wasn't too proud to come and see old Granny Peckham and say how cut up he was about poor Dawnie. He come in a big gold car and he kissed me and brought me a two-pound box of Black Magic.' Her eyes gleamed greedily at the thought of the chocolates, waiting for her perhaps in her bedroom. She sighed contentedly. 'I'll get off for me lay-down now,' she said.

10

The Burden children were old enough now to come home to an empty house and get their own tea, but more often they went straight from school to the house of their Aunt Grace, and in the holidays Pat Burden spent most of her time there, playing with the baby. Her brother led the marauding life of a teenage boy, wandering with a small gang of contemporaries in the fields, fishing in the Kingsbrook or playing the jukebox at the Carousel café. Burden knew very well that his son's life would have differed very little from this pattern even if there had been a mother at the bungalow in Tabard Road. He understood that a girl child needs an adult female on whom to model herself and he knew that she had that in Grace. But he worried incessantly about his children. Would John become a delinquent if he were out after nine in the evening? Would Pat carry a trauma through life because at the age of thirteen she was occasionally expected to open a tin or make tea? Did he give them too much pocket money or not enough? Ought he, for their sakes, to marry again? Innocent of any, he was loaded down with guilt.

He went to absurd lengths to ensure that neither of them had to do any work they would not have done had his wife lived. For this reason he was always taking them out to meals or rushing home with packages of expensive frozen food. Pat must never walk the half-mile from Grace's house to Tabard Road. He would have let her walk it without a thought if Jean had lived. But motherless children had to be fetched in father's car. He suffered agonies of frustration and recrimination if he was busy on a case and Pat had to wait an hour or even be abandoned to her aunt for an evening.

Wexford knew this. Whereas he would never excuse Burden from essential work on these grounds, he regretfully gave up the practice of detaining the inspector after hours to sit with him in the Olive and Dove and thrash out some current problem. Burden was worse than useless as a participant in these discussions. His eyes were always on the clock. Every drink he had was 'one for the road', and from time to time he would start from his seat and express the worry uppermost in his mind. Had John come in yet?

But old habits die hard. Wexford preferred the atmosphere in the Olive to the adolescent-ruled, untidy living room of the bungalow. He felt guilty when Pat was prevented from doing her ballet exercises and John had to turn off the record player, but he had to talk to Burden sometimes, discuss things with him outside hours. As he came to the door that evening, he heard the pom-pom, the roar and the whine of pop music before he rang the bell.

Burden was in his shirt sleeves, a plastic apron round his waist. He took this off hurriedly when he saw who his caller was. 'Just finishing the dishes,' he said. 'I'll nip out for some beer, shall I?'

'No need. I've brought it. What did you think I'd got in the bag? More treasures from the river? Who's the vocalist, John?'

'Zeno Vedast,' said John reverently. He looked at his father. 'I suppose I'll have to turn it off now.'

'Not on my account,' said Wexford. 'I rather like his voice.'

Vedast wasn't singing any of the festival songs but an older hit which had for so long been number one in the charts that even Wexford had heard it. Once or twice he had heard himself humming the melody. It was a gentle folk song about a country wedding.

'Dad's going to buy me the Sundays album for my birthday.'

'That'll set you back a bit, Mike.'

'Six quid,' said Burden gloomily.

'I wonder if any of these songs will live? We tend to forget that some of the greatest songs were pop in their day. After *The Marriage of Figaro* was first performed in the seventeen-eighties, they say Mozart heard the errand boys whistling *Non piu andrai* in the streets of Vienna. And it's still popular.'

'Oh, yes?' said Burden politely and uncomprehendingly. 'You can turn it off now, John. Mr Wexford didn't come round here to talk about Zeno Vedast or Goodbody or whatever his name is.'

'That's just what I did come for.' Wexford went into the kitchen and picked up a tea towel. He began polishing glasses, resisting Burden's efforts to stop him. 'I've a feeling that before we go any further we ought to see Dawn's lion, the lion who roars like any sucking dove.'

'Wherever he may be at this moment.'

'That's no problem, Mike. He's here. Or, at any rate, he's at the Cheriton Forest Hotel.' Wexford drank the half-pint Burden had poured out for him and told the inspector about his talk with Mrs Peckham. 'I don't know that it means much. He may make a point of visiting old ladies rather on the lines of a parliamentary candidate nursing babies. Never neglect any opportunity of currying favour and influencing people. Or he may be an ordinary nice bloke who wanted to condole with the dead girl's grandma. It certainly doesn't mean he'd seen Dawn recently.'

John put his head round the door. 'I'm going out, Dad.'

Burden began to flap. 'Where? Why? What d'you want to go out now for?'

'Only down the Carousel.'

Wexford said smoothly, 'That's fine, John, because we're going out too. Your father won't be back till ten-thirty, so you'd better have the key. You're bound to be in before him, aren't you?'

Burden handed over the key in meek stupefaction and John took it as if it were something precious and wonderful. When the boy had gone—rapidly before there could be any changes of heart—Burden said suspiciously, 'You talked to him exactly as if he were grown-up.'

'Don't have any more beer, Mike. I want you to drive us.'

'To Cheriton Forest, I suppose?'

'Mm-hm. Vedast's dining in tonight. I checked.' Wexford looked at his watch. 'He ought to have just about finished his dinner.'

'Oh God. I don't know. Pat's at Grace's. John . . .'

'The boy's glad you're going out. It was a relief. Couldn't you see that? You won't go out for his sake. D'you want him to get so he can't go out for yours?'

'I sometimes think human relationships are impossible. Communication's impossible.'

'And you're a fool,' said Wexford, but he said it affectionately.

Cheriton Forest, a large fir plantation, lies some two miles to the south of Kingsmarkham. It is intersected by a number of sandy rides and one metalled road on which, in a big heathy clearing, is situated the Cheriton Forest Hotel.

This is a newer and far more fashionable hotel than the Olive and Dove in Kingsmarkham. The original building, put up in the thirties, is supposed to be a copy of a Tudor manor house. But there are too many beams and studs, the plaster is too white and the beams too black, the woodwork a decoration rather than an integral part of the structure. And the whole thing which might have mellowed with time has been vulgarised by a vast glass cocktail bar and by rows of motel bungalows added on in the late sixties.

When Wexford and Burden arrived at the hotel it was still

broad daylight, a dull summer evening, windy and cool. The wind stirred the forest trees, ruffling them against a pale sky where grey clouds, rimmed in the west with pink, moved, gathered, lost their shapes, torn by the wind.

On a Saturday night the forecourt would by this time have been crammed with cars and the cocktail bar full of people. But this was mid-week. Through a mullioned window a few sedate diners could be seen at tables, waiters moving unhurriedly with trays. This dining-room window was closed as were all the others in the building except one on the floor above, a pair of french windows giving on to a balcony which was quite out of keeping with the design of the hotel. The wind sent these diamond-paned glass doors banging shut and bursting open again, and from time to time it caught the velvet curtains, beating them, making them toss like washing on a line.

There was plenty of room in the parking bays for the half-dozen vehicles which stood there. Only one was on the fore-court proper, a golden Rolls-Royce parked askew, the silver gable of its grid nosing into a flower-bed and crushing geranium blossoms.

Wexford stared at this car from the windows of his own which Burden was steering, with rule-abiding propriety, into a vacant bay. He had heard of the fashion of covering the bodywork of cars in a furry coating to seem like skin or coarse velvet, but he had never yet seen this done in use, except in glossy advertisements. The Rolls wore a skin of pale golden fur, the vibrant sand colour of a lion's pelt which gleamed softly and richly, and on its bonnet, just above the grid, was attached a statuette of a plunging lion that seemed to be made of solid gold.

'This beast-of-prey motif keeps cropping up,' he said. He approached the car to get a closer look and as he did so the driver's door opened and a girl got out. It was Nell Tate.

'Good evening,' he said. 'We've met before.'

'I don't think so. I don't remember.' It was the voice of a person accustomed to defending a celebrity from intrusive fans.

'At the festival.' Wexford introduced himself and Burden. 'I'd like a word with Mr Vedast.'

Nell Tate looked seriously alarmed. 'You can't see Zeno. He's resting. He's probably asleep. We're all trying to get a quiet evening. I only came down to get something out of the car.'

She looked as if she were in need of rest. Beautifully dressed in a long clinging gown of silver lace under which she obviously wore nothing at all, heavy platinum ornaments at neck and wrists, she had a look of hag-ridden exhaustion. Under the silver and purple paint, her left eye was very swollen, the white of it bloodshot between puffy, painful lids. Studying it covertly, Wexford thought that considerable courage must have been needed to stick false lashes on to that bruised membrane.

'There's no hurry,' he said smoothly. 'We'll wait. Are you in the motel?'

'Oh, no.' She had a false poise that was growing brittle. 'We've got what they call the Elizabethan suite. Can you give me some idea what it's about?'

'Dawn Stonor. Tell him we want to talk to him about Dawn Stonor.'

She didn't even go through the pretence of looking bewildered or asking who this was. 'I'll tell him. Couldn't you come back tomorrow?'

'I think we'll wait,' said Wexford. He and Burden followed her into the foyer of the hotel, a porter having sprung forward to open the door for her. Observing the way she swept past the man, her head going up and her shoulders wriggling, passing him without a word or a nod, Wexford hardened his heart. 'We'll give you a quarter of an hour and then we'll come up.'

She made for the lift. The spurned porter, not at all put out,

92

watched her admiringly. Once in the lift, before the doors closed on her, she appeared multiplied three times by the mirrors which lined its walls. Four blonde girls in silver, four bruised eyes, glared at Wexford and then the doors closed and she was whisked upwards.

'Lovely,' said the porter feelingly.

'What are they doing here?'

'Mr Vedast's here to purchase a country property, sir.'

Anyone else, thought Wexford, would have just bought a house. He fished for a couple of coins and found only a fifty-pence piece. 'Any luck, yet?'

'Thank you very much, sir. They go out looking every day, sir, him and Mr and Mrs Tate. We've had a few fans outside but they didn't have no joy on account of Mr Vedast takes all his meals in his suite.'

'She was scared stiff when you said who we were,' said Burden when the porter had gone out of earshot.

'I know, but that may be only that she's afraid of having him disturbed. I wonder if it was he who gave her that black eye?'

'More likely her husband, poor devil. That's a *ménage à trois* if ever there was one. D'you think there are two bedrooms or only one in that suite?'

'For a self-avowed puritan, Mike, you take a very lubricious interest in these things. Here you are, get your nose into *Nova* and you can pass me *The Field*.'

For fifteen minutes they leafed through the glossy periodicals provided in the Shakespeare Lounge. A very old couple came in and switched on the television. When they were satisfied that it was glowing with colour and braying forth cricket scores, they ignored it and began to read novels. A Dalmatian entered, wandered about and fell into a despairing heap in front of the cold electric heater.

'Right, time's up,' said Wexford. 'Now for the lion's den.'

11

The suite was on the first floor. They were admitted not by Nell but by a small dark man of about thirty who introduced himself as Godfrey Tate and who favoured them with a narrow smile. There was something spare and economical about him from his longish thin black hair and dab of moustache to his tiny feet in lace-up boots. He wore tube-like black slacks, a very tight skimpy black shirt, and the air of one who rations his movements, his speech and his manners to the starkest barrenness social usage permits.

'Zeno can spare you ten minutes.'

They were in a small entrance hall filled with flowers, displays of roses, sweet peas and stephanotis, whose perfume hung cloyingly on the air. Burden knocked a rosebud out of a vase and cursed softly. The living room was large and not at all Elizabethan, being done up in the style of a provincial casino with panels of pink mirror on the walls, niches containing more flowers in gilt urns, and french windows, hung with velvet and opening on to a balcony. In here the atmosphere was not stuffy or soporific. All the doors were open, showing a bathroom whose floor was cluttered with wet towels, and the interiors of two bedrooms, one containing a huge double bed and the other two singles. All had been occupied until recently as the tumbled bedclothes showed, but as to who had occupied which and with whom it was impossible to tell. Both bedrooms, like the living room, were littered all over with discarded clothes, magazines, records, and suitcases spilling out their contents. A lusty gale blew through the open windows, shaking the flowers and making the curtains billow and thrash.

Nell Tate looked blue with cold, her arms spiky with goose-flesh. Not so her companion, who, bare-chested, sat at a table by the window eating roast duck with the enthusiasm of one who has been brought up on baked beans.

'Good evening, Mr Vedast. I'm sorry to disturb your dinner.'

Vedast didn't get up, but his hairless, polished-looking face, all bones and almost Slavonic planes, split into a wide grin. 'Hallo. Good evening. Have some coffee.' His voice had no affectations. It was still what it must have always been, the local mixture of Sussex burr and mild cockney. 'Make them send up more coffee, Nello, and take all this away.' He made a sweeping gesture with his arm, indicating the two other plates on which the food had only been picked at, the covered dishes, the basket of melba toast. 'Phone down now. Go on.' No one had touched the cream trifle. Vedast took the whole bowl and set it in his lap.

'Maybe they'd rather have a drink,' said Godfrey Tate.

'You mean *you* would, Goffo. Didn't you know they're not allowed to drink on duty?' Spooning up trifle, Vedast grinned at Wexford. He had an ugly attractive face, *joli laid*, very white and oddly bare. His eyes were a light, clear brown that sometimes looked yellow. 'The trouble with Nello and Goffo,' he said, 'is that they never read. They're not informed. Get on with your phoning and drinking, dears.'

Like discontented slaves, the Tates did his bidding. Tate took an almost empty bottle of brandy from a pseudo Louis Quinze cabinet and tipped what remained of it into a glass. He stood drinking it and watching his wife darkly while she phoned down for more coffee. Vedast laughed.

'Why don't you sit down? Not too cold in here, is it?' He put out his hand to Nell and beckoned her, pursing his lips into a whistle shape. She came up to him eagerly, too eagerly.

She was trembling with cold. It was all she could do to stop her teeth from chattering. 'Fresh air is good for Nello and Goffo. If I didn't look after their health they'd be like two little broiler chickens, shut up all day in hot hutches. I think we'll do our house-hunting on foot tomorrow, Nello.'

'Then you can count me out,' said Tate.

'Must we? You won't mind if Nello comes with me, will you?' Emaciated, starved-looking, Vedast finished the dessert which had been intended for three people. 'Perhaps our visitors can tell us of all sorts of lovely houses going spare round here?'

'We aren't house agents, Mr Vedast,' said Burden, 'and we've come to ask you questions, not answer them.'

The coffee arrived before Vedast could reply to this. Tate took one look at it, swallowed his drink and searched in the cupboard for a fresh bottle of brandy. While his wife poured coffee, he found a bottle tucked away at the back and quite full though already opened. A liberal measure in his glass, he took a long deep draught.

Immediately he was convulsed, choking and clapping one hand over his mouth.

'Christ!' A dribble of liquid came out through his fingers. 'That's not brandy! What the hell is it?'

Vedast laughed, his head on one side. 'Meths and cold tea, Goffo. Just a little experiment to see if you could tell the difference.' Nell giggled, squeezed close against Vedast's side. 'I poured the brandy down the loo. Best place for it.'

Tate said nothing. He went into the bathroom and slammed the door.

'Poor little man! Never mind, we'll take him out to dinner tomorrow at that lovely place in Pomfret. Kiss, Nello? That's right. No hard feelings because I like playing tricks on your old man? How is your coffee, Chief Inspector?'

'Well, it *is* coffee, Mr Vedast. Apparently one runs a risk drinking in your establishment.'

'I wouldn't dare doctor your coffee. I've a great respect for the law.'

'Good,' said Wexford drily. 'I hope you've enough respect to tell me what was your relationship with Dawn Stonor.'

For a moment Vedast was silent but he didn't seem disturbed. He was waiting while Nell poured cream into his cup and then added four lumps of sugar.

'Thank you, Nello darling. Now you run away and paint something. Your poor eye, for instance.'

'Do I have to?' said Nell like a child who has been told she must go to the dentist.

'Of course you do when Zeno says so. The quicker you go the sooner it will all be over. Run along.'

She ran along. She wasn't a child but a grown woman, shivering with cold and with a black eye. Vedast smiled indulgently. He walked to the bathroom door and paused, listening to Tate running taps and brushing his teeth. Then he came back, kicking shut the door of the drinks cabinet as he passed it, and stretched himself out full-length on the pink velvet sofa.

'You wanted to ask me about Dawnie,' he said. 'I suppose you've been talking to Mummy Stonor or even Granny Peckham?'

'They say you were at school with Dawn.'

'So I was. So were ever such a lot of other people. Why pick on me?'

'Mr Vedast,' said Wexford heavily, 'Dawn told her flatmate that you and she had remained friends since you left school, and she told her grandmother that you took her out to dinner on the Friday before she died. We know that can't have been true since you were in Manchester that day, but we'd like to know how well you knew Dawn and when you last saw her.'

Vedast took a lump of sugar and sucked it. He seemed completely relaxed, one leg casually crossed over the other.

Still in their raincoats, Wexford and Burden were not even comfortably warm, but Vedast, almost naked, showed no sign of being affected by the cold damp wind. The golden hairs on his chest lay flat under the light gold chain which hung against them.

'When we both lived here,' he said, 'she was my girl friend.'

'You mean you were lovers?'

Vedast nodded, smiling pleasantly. 'I was her first lover. We were sixteen. Rather moving, don't you think? Martin Silk discovered me and all sorts of exciting things happened to me which wouldn't interest you at all. Dawnie and I lost touch. I didn't see her again till this year.'

'Where did you see her?'

'In the Townsman Club,' said Vedast promptly. 'Nello and Goffo and I went there as guests of a friend of mine, and there was Dawnie serving drinks. My poor little Dawnie in a yellow satin corset and tights! I nearly laughed but that would have been unkind. She came and sat down at our table and we had a long chat about old times. She even remembered what I like to drink, orange juice with sugar in it.'

'Did you communicate with her after that?'

'Just once.' Vedast spoke very lightly, very easily, his fingers playing with the gold chain. 'Nello and Goffo had gone away to see Goffo's mum and I was rather lonely, all on my own and sad, you know.' He smiled, the unspoilt star, the poor little rich boy. 'Dawnie had written down her phone number for me at the club. Nello didn't like that a bit, you can imagine. I thought, why not give Dawnie a ring?'

'And did you?'

'Of course I did.' Now Vedast's smile was apologetic, a little rueful, the smile of the unspoilt star who longs for the companions of his humbler days to treat him as the simple country boy he really is at heart. 'But it's very off-putting, isn't it, when people sort of swamp you? D'you know what I mean? When they're terribly enthusiastic, sort of fawning?'

'You mean you got bored?' said Burden bluntly.

'It sounds unkind, put that way. Let's say I thought it better not to revive something which was dead and gone. Sorry, that wasn't very tactful. What I mean is I choked Dawnie off. I said it would be lovely if we could meet again sometime, but I was so busy at present.'

'When did this telephone conversation take place, Mr Vedast?'

'Three or four weeks ago. It was just a little chat, leading to nothing. Fancy Dawnie telling Granny Peckham we'd met! Nello and Goffo could tell you when it was they went away.' He fixed his cat's eyes, yellowish, narrow, on Wexford, opening them very wide suddenly, and again they had a sharp sly glint. 'And they'll tell you where I was on June sixth. I know that'll be the next thing you'll ask.'

'Where were you, Mr Vedast?'

'At my house in Duvette Gardens, South Kensington. Nello and Goffo and I were all there. We came back from Manchester during the Sunday night and just lazed about and slept all that Monday. Here's Goffo, all clean and purified. He'll tell you.'

Godfrey Tate had emerged from the bathroom, blankfaced, contained, wary, but showing no grudge against Vedast for the humiliating trick to which the singer had subjected him.

'Who's taking my name in vain?' he said with an almost pathetically unsuccessful attempt at jocularity.

'Tell the officers where I was on June sixth, Goffo.'

'With me and Nell.' He responded so promptly, so glibly, that it was evident the stating of this alibi had been rehearsed. 'We were all together in Duvette Gardens all day and all night. Nell can tell you the same. Nell!'

Wexford was sure she had been listening behind the door, for she exclaimed when her husband opened it as if she had been knocked backwards.

'Of course we were all there,' she said. She had covered her-

99

self with a long coat but she was still cold and she moved towards the window as if to close it. When Vedast, still smiling, shook his head, she sat down obediently, huddled in the coat, and at a glance from him, said, 'We didn't go out all day. We were exhausted after Manchester.' One hand went up to the sore eye, hovered and fell again into her lap.

'And now,' said the singer, 'tell the officers when you went off on your trip to see Goffo's mum.'

If Tate had had a tail, Wexford thought, he would at this point have wagged it. Rather like a performing dog who loves yet fears his master and who is utterly hypnotised by him, he sat up, raised his head eagerly.

'About a month ago, wasn't it?' prompted Vedast.

'We went on May twenty-second,' said Nell, 'and . . .'

'Came back on Wednesday, the twenty-fifth,' her husband ended for her.

Vedast looked pleased. For a moment it looked as if he would pat his dogs on their heads, but instead he smiled at Tate and blew a kiss at Tate's wife. 'You see, Chief Inspector? We lead a very quiet life. I didn't kill Dawnie out of passion, Goffo didn't kill her because I told him to—though I'm sure he would have done if I had—and Nello didn't kill her out of jealousy. So we can't help you. We've got masses of stuff from agents to look through tonight, so may we get on with our house-hunting?'

'Yes, Mr Vedast, you may, but I can't promise I shan't want to see you again.'

Vedast sprang to his feet in one supple movement. 'No, don't promise. I should love to see you again. We've had such a nice talk. We don't see many people, we have to be so careful.' Wexford's hand was cordially shaken. 'See them out, Goffo, and lock up the car.'

'I wish you good hunting, Mr Vedast,' said Wexford.

John Burden was at home and already in bed, having left a

note for his father to tell him that Pat would be staying the night with her aunt. The key had been left under a flower-pot, which shocked the policeman in Burden while the father showed a fatuous pride in his son's forethought. He removed the Vedast L.P. from the turntable and closed the record player.

'One of these songs,' he said, 'is called "Whistle and I'll come to you, my love".'

'Very appropriate.' Wexford glanced at the record sleeve. 'He must have written that for the Tates' theme song.'

'My God, yes. Why do they put up with it?'

'She for love, he for money. Both for the reflected glory. He hit the nail right on the head when he said "Goffo" would have killed Dawn if he'd told him to. They'd do anything for him. "Being your slave, what should I do but tend upon the hours and times of your desire?" It's not just love and money and glory, but the power of the man's personality. It's sinister, it's most unpleasant. In a set-up of this kind that alibi goes for nothing. An alibi supported by slaves is no alibi. The Romans in their heyday were very chary about admitting slaves' evidence.'

Burden chuckled. 'I daresay you're right, Caesar. How did he know he needed an alibi for the sixth of June, anyway? We didn't tell him.'

'Mrs Stonor or Mrs Peckham may have told him. There was something about it in the papers, about our thinking that the probable date of her death. I don't really suppose he's involved at all. He likes playing with us, that's all. He likes sailing near the wind. Above all, he enjoys frightening the others.' Wexford added in the words of the Duke of Wellington: ' "By God, he frightens me!" '

12

The interior decorations of Leonard Dunsand's bungalow were precisely the same as those of Miss Mowler's. Identical red spotted paper covered the hall walls, identical birds and lilies pained the eye in the living room. But Miss Mowler, for all her genteel shudders at the builder's bad taste, had shown little more judgment in her own and had filled the place with garish furniture and mass-produced pictures. Dunsand's drab pieces, brown leather smoking-room chairs, late Victorian tables and, above all, shelf upon shelf of scholarly books, looked absurdly incongruous here. Little shrivelled cacti, lifeless greenish-brown pin-cushions, stood in pots on the window-sills. There was nothing in the hall but a bare mahogany table and no carpet on the floor. It was the typical home of the celibate intellectual, uncharacteristic only in that it was as clean as Mrs Peveril's and that, on a table in the living room, lay a stack of holiday brochures, their covers even more vividly coloured than the wallpaper.

Dunsand, who had just come home from work, asked them to sit down in a colourless but cultivated voice. He seemed about forty with thinning mousey hair and rubbery face whose features were too puffy for that tight mouth. Thick glasses distorted his eyes, making them appear protuberant. He wore an immaculate, extremely conventional dark suit, white shirt and dark tie. Neither obstructive nor ingratiating, he repeated what he had already told Burden, that he had reached home at about six-forty on June sixth and had noticed no unusual happenings in The Pathway during that evening.

'I prepared myself a meal,' he said, 'and then I did some housework. This place is very ugly inside but I see no reason why it should also be dirty.'

'Did you see anything of your neighbours?'

'I saw Mrs Peveril go down the road at half past seven. I understand she attends an evening class in some sort of handicraft.'

'You didn't go out yourself? It was a fine evening.'

'Was it?' said Dunsand politely. 'No, I didn't go out.'

'Are you on friendly terms with your neighbours, Mr Dunsand?'

'Oh, yes, very.'

'You go into their houses, for instance? They visit you?'

'No. I think I misunderstood you. I simply mean we nod to each other and say a word if we meet in the street.'

Wexford sighed to himself. He found Dunsand depressing and he pitied his students. Philosophy, he knew—although he knew little about it—is not all ethics, witty syllogisms, anecdotes about Pythagoras, but logic, abstruse mathematics, points and instants, epistemological premisses. Imagine this one holding forth for a couple of hours on Wittgenstein!

'So you can tell us nothing of Mr and Mrs Peveril's way of life, their habits, who calls on them and so on?'

'No, nothing.' Dunsand spoke in the same drab level voice, but Wexford fancied that for a brief moment he had caught a certain animation in the man's eye, a sign of life, a flash perhaps of pain. It was gone, the magnified eyes were still and staring. 'I think I can say, Chief Inspector, that I know nothing of any private life but my own.'

'And that is ... ?' Wexford said hesitantly.

'What you see.' Dunsand cleared his throat. 'Beginning to rain again,' he said. 'If you don't want to ask me anything else I'll go and put my car away.'

'Do you ever go to London, Mr Peveril?'

'Of course I do in connection with my work.' Peveril put a

gloomy and irritable emphasis on the last word. He had once more been fetched from his studio and his fingers were actually inky. Wexford couldn't help feeling that the ink had been put there deliberately just as the man's hair had been purposely shaken and made to stand up in awry spikes. 'I go up occasionally, once a fortnight, once a month.'

'And stay overnight?'

'I have done.'

'When did you last go?'

'Oh God, it would have been June first, I think. I didn't stay.' Peveril glanced towards the closed door which excluded his wife. 'Scenes,' he said stiffly, 'are made if I venture to spend a night away from the matrimonial nest.' Misanthropic, his whole manner showing how distasteful he found this probing, he nevertheless was unable to resist making frank disclosures. 'You'd imagine that a woman who has everything soft and easy for her, never earned a penny since she found someone to keep her, wouldn't deny the breadwinner a few hours of freedom. But there it is. If I go to London I have to phone her when I get there and leave a number for her to call me whenever she fancies, that means about three times in one evening.'

Wexford shrugged. It was not an uncommon type of marriage that Peveril had described; he was only one of many who had elected to make the dreariest and the longest journey with a jealous foe. But why talk about it? Because it would induce his interrogator to believe that such surveillance kept him from other women? Wexford almost smiled at such naivety. He knew that good-looking, dissatisfied men of Peveril's stamp, childless men long out of love with their wives, could be Houdini-like in the facility with which they escaped from domestic bonds. He left the subject.

'Your wife went to an evening class on that Monday evening,' he said. 'Would you mind telling me what your movements were?'

104

'I *moved* into my studio to work and I didn't *move* out of it until my wife got back at eleven.'

'There are no buses at that time of night. She didn't take your car?'

An edge of contempt to his voice, Peveril said, 'She can't drive. She walked into Kingsmarkham and some woman gave her a lift back.'

'You didn't think of driving her, then? It was a fine evening and it isn't far.'

'Damn it all!' said Peveril, his ready temper rising. 'Why the hell should I drive her to some daft hen party where they don't learn a bloody thing? It's not as if she was going to work, going to bring in some much-needed money.' He added sullenly, 'I usually do drive her, as a matter of fact.'

'Why didn't you that night?'

'The worm turned,' said Peveril. 'That's why not. Now I'd appreciate it if you'd let me get on with my work.'

It was on the red dress that Wexford concentrated that Friday. He called a semi-informal conference consisting of himself, Burden, Dr Crocker, Sergeant Martin and Detective Polly Davies. They sat in his office, their chairs in a circle, with the dress laid on his desk. Then Wexford decided that for them all to get a better view of it while they talked, the best thing would be to hang it from the ceiling. A hanger was produced by Polly, and dress and hanger suspended from the lead of Wexford's central light.

Laboratory experts had subjected it to a thorough examination. They had found that it was made of synthetic fibre and that it had been frequently worn probably by the same person, a brown-haired, fair-skinned Caucasian. There were no sweat stains in the armpits. In the fibre had been found traces of an unidentified perfume, talcum powder, anti-perspirant and carbon tetrachloride, a cleaning fluid. Other researches showed the dress to have been manufactured some eight or nine years previously at a North London factory for distribution by a small fashion house that dealt in medium-priced clothes. It might have been bought in London, Manchester, Birmingham or a host of other towns and cities in the British Isles. No Kingsmarkham store had ever stocked the garments from this fashion house, but they were, and had for a long time been, obtainable in Brighton.

The dress itself was a dark purplish red, darker than magenta and bluer than burgundy. It had a plain round neck, three-quarter-length sleeves, a fitted waist with self belt and a skirt designed just to show the wearer's knees. This indicated that it had been bought for a woman about five feet seven inches tall, a woman who was also, but not exceptionally, slim, for it was a size twelve. On Dawn Stonor it had been a tight fit and an unfashionable length for this or any other epoch.

'Comments, please,' said Wexford. 'You first, Polly. You look as if you've got something to say.'

'Well, sir, I was just thinking that she must have looked really grotty in it.' Polly was a lively, black-haired young woman who habitually dressed in the 'dolly' mode, mini-skirts, natty waistcoats and velvet baker-boy caps. Her way of painting her mouth strawberry red and blotching two red dabs on her cheeks made her look less intelligent than she was. Now she saw from Wexford's frown that her imprecise epithet had displeased him and she corrected herself hurriedly. 'I mean, it wouldn't have suited her and she'd have looked dowdy and awful. A real freak. I know that sounds unkind—of course she looked dreadful when she was found—but what I'm try-ing to say is that she must have looked dreadful from the moment she put it on.'

'You'd say, would you, that the dress itself is unattractive as a garment? I'm asking you particularly, Polly, because you're a woman and more likely to see these things than we are.'

'It's so hard to say, sir, when something's gone out of date. I suppose with jewellery and so forth it might have looked all right on a dark person it fitted well. It wouldn't have looked good on Dawn because she had sort of reddish-blonde hair and she must have absolutely bulged out of it. I can't think she'd ever have put it on from *choice*. And another thing, sir, you said I'm more likely to notice these things than you are, but—well, just for an experiment, could you all say what you think of it as, say, a dress you'd like your wives to wear?'

'Anything you say. Doctor?'

Crocker uncrossed his elegant legs and put his head on one side. 'It's a bit difficult,' he began, 'to separate it from the unpleasant associations it has, but I'll try. It's rather *dull*. Let me say that if my wife wore it I'd feel she wasn't letting me down in any way. I wouldn't mind who saw her in it. It's got what I believe they call an "uncluttered line" and it would show off a woman's figure in a discreet kind of way. On the other hand, supposing I was the sort of man who took other women out, I don't think I'd feel any too thrilled if my girl friend turned up to a date wearing it because it wouldn't be—well, adventurous enough.'

'Mike?'

Burden had no wife, but he had come to terms with his condition. He was able to talk of wives now without inner pain or outward embarrassment. 'I agree with the doctor that it's rather distasteful to imagine anyone close to you wearing it because of the circumstances and so on associated with it. When I make myself look at it as I might look at a dress in a shop window I'd say I rather like it. No doubt, I've no idea of fashion, but I'd call it smart. If I were—er, a married man I'd like to see my wife in it.'

'Sergeant?'

'It's a smart dress, sir,' said Martin eagerly. 'My wife's got a dress rather like it and that sort of shade. I bought it for her last Christmas, chose it myself, come to that. My daughter—she's twenty-two—she says she wouldn't be seen dead in it, but you know these young girls—beg your pardon, Polly. That's a nice, smart dress, sir, or was.'

'Now for me,' said Wexford. 'I like it. It looks comfortable and practical for everyday wear. One would feel pleasantly uxorious and somehow secure sitting down in the evening with a woman in that dress. And I think it would be becoming on the right person. As the doctor says, it follows the natural lines of a woman's figure. It's not daring or dramatic or embarrassing. It's conservative. There you are, Polly. What do you make of all that?'

Polly laughed. 'It tells me more about all you than the dress,' she said pertly. 'But what it does tell me is that it's a *man's* dress, sir. I mean, it's the sort of thing a man would choose because it's figure-flattering and plain and somehow, as you said, secure. Dr Crocker said he wouldn't want to see his girl friend in it. Doesn't all this mean it's a *wife's* dress chosen by a *husband* partly because he subconsciously realises it shows she's a good little married lady and any other man seeing her in it will know she's not made of girl-friend stuff?'

'Perhaps it does,' said Wexford thoughtfully. The window was open and the dress swayed and swivelled in the breeze. Find the owner, he thought, and then I have all I need to know. 'That's intelligent of you, Polly, but where does it get us? You've convinced me it was owned at one time by a married woman who bought it to please her husband. We already know Dawn didn't own it. Its owner might have sent it to a jumble sale, given it to her cleaner or taken it to the Oxfam shop.'

'We could check with the Oxfam people here, sir.'

'Yes, Sergeant, that must be done. I believe you said, Mike, that Mrs Peveril denies ownership?'

'She may be lying. When it was shown to her I thought she

was going to faint. With that stain on it it isn't a particularly attractive object and there are, as we've said, the associations. But she reacted to it very strongly. On the other hand, we know she's a nervy and hysterical woman. It could be a natural reaction.'

'Have you talked to Mrs Clarke again?'

'She says her friend had some sort of mental breakdown last year and lost a lot of weight, so it hardly looks as if she was ever slim enough to wear the dress. But Mrs Clarke has only known her four years.'

'Eight years ago,' Wexford said thoughtfully, 'the Peverils might still have been on romantic terms. He might have been choosing clothes for her that were particularly to his taste. But I agree with you that the question of size makes that unlikely. Well, I won't detain you any longer. It's a massive plan I've got in mind, but I think it's the only course to take. Somehow or other we're going to have to question every woman in Kingsmarkham and Stowerton between the ages of thirty and sixty, show them the dress and get reactions. Ask each one if it's hers or, if not, whether she's ever seen anyone else wearing it.'

His announcement was received with groans by all but the doctor, who left quickly, declaring that his presence was needed at the infirmary.

13

The response to Wexford's appeal was enormous and immediate. Women queued up outside the Baptist church hall to view the dress as they might have queued on the first day of a significant sale. Public-spirited? Wexford thought their enthusiasm sprang more from a need to seem for a little while important. People like to be caught up in the whirlwind of something sensational and they like it even more if, instead of being part of a crowd, each can for a brief moment be an individual, noticed, attended to, taken seriously. They like to leave their names and addresses, see themselves recorded. He supposed they also liked to feast their eyes on the relic of a violent act. Was it so bad if they did? Was it what the young festival visitors would have called sick? Or was it rather evidence of a strong human vitality, the curiosity that wants to see everything, know everything, be in the swim, that when refined and made scholarly, is the prerogative of the historian and the archaeologist?

He had long ago ceased to allow hope to triumph over experience. He didn't suppose that some woman would come forward and say her husband had unexpectedly and inexplicably borrowed the dress from her that Monday evening. Nor did he anticipate any dramatic scene in the hall, a wife screaming or falling into a faint because she recognised the dress and realised simultaneously what recognition implied. No woman harbouring a guilty secret would come there voluntarily. But he did hope for something. Someone would say she had seen the garment on a friend or an acquaintance; someone would admit to having possessed it and then to have given it away or sold it.

No one did. All Friday afternoon they filed along the wooden passage that smelt of hymn books and Boy Scouts, passed into the grim brown hall to sit on the Women's Fellowship chairs and stare at the posters for coffee mornings and social evenings. Then, one by one, they went behind the screens where Martin and Polly had the dress laid out on a trestle table. One by one they came out with the baulked, rather irritable, look on their faces of do-gooders whom ill-luck had robbed of the chance to be more than negatively helpful.

'I suppose,' said Burden, 'that she could have been picked up by a man in a car. A prearranged pick-up, of course. He might have come from anywhere.'

'In that case, why take a bus to Sundays and walk across the fields? Mrs Peveril says she saw her go into those fields and her description is so accurate that I think we must believe her. Dawn may have been early for her date—that was the only bus as we've said before—gone into the fields to sit down and wait, and then doubled back. But if she did that, she didn't go far back.'

'What makes you say that?'

'Four people saw her between the time she left her mother's house and the time she went into those fields, five-thirty. We've not been able to find anyone who saw her *after* five-thirty, though God knows we've made enough appeals and questioned enough people. Therefore it's almost certain she went into some house somewhere just after five-thirty.'

Burden frowned. 'On the Sundays estate, you mean?'

'To put it more narrowly than that, in The Pathway. The body was in the quarry, Mike. It was carried or dragged to the quarry, not transported in a car. You know what a job it was to get our own cars down there. When the gates to the drive are locked no car could get in.' Wexford glanced at his watch.

111

'It's five-thirty and the Olive's open. Can't we leave Martin to carry on with this and adjourn for a drink? I'd rather talk all this out sitting down over a pint.'

Burden's brow creased further and he bit his lip. 'What about Pat? She'll have to get her own tea. She'll have to walk to her dancing lesson. John'll be all alone.'

In a tone that is usually described as patient but which, in fact indicates an extreme degree of controlled exasperation, Wexford said, 'He is six feet tall. He is fifteen. By the time he was that age my old dad had been out at work eighteen months. Why can't he escort his sister to her dancing class? Taking it for granted, of course, that if she walks three hundred yards alone on a bright summer evening, she's bound to be set on by kidnappers.'

'I'll phone them,' said Burden with a shamefaced grin.

The saloon bar of the Olive and Dove was almost empty, a little gloomy and uninviting as deserted low-ceilinged places always are when the sun shines brightly outside. Wexford carried their drinks into the garden where wooden tables and chairs were arranged under an arbour. Vines and clematises made a leafy roof over their heads. It was the home-going hour, the time when the peace and the quiet of this spot was usually shattered by the sound of brakes and shifting gears as traffic poured over the Kingsbrook bridge.

Today all man-made noise was drowned by the chatter of the swollen river running beside the terraced garden. It was a steady low roar, constant and unchanging, but like all natural sound it was neither tedious to the ear nor a hindrance to conversation. It was soothing. It spoke of timeless forces, pure and untameable, which in a world of ugliness and violence resisted man's indifferent soiling of the earth. Listening to it, sitting in silence, Wexford thought of that ugliness, the scheme of things in which a girl could be beaten to death, thrown into a bower which had been made and used for love, thrown like garbage.

He shivered. He could never quite get used to it, the appalling things that happened, the waste, the pointlessness. But now he had to think of practical matters, of why and how this particular ugliness had taken place, and when Burden came to the table he said:

'You've talked to the occupants of the other two houses in The Pathway and I haven't. Would you say we could exclude them?'

'The Streets are a married couple with four children, all of whom were at home with their parents the whole evening. None of them saw Dawn. Mrs Street saw Miss Mowler come home at eight o'clock. Apart from that, none of them saw any of their neighbours that evening. They heard nothing and they remained in the front of the house from about six till about ten. Mrs Street's kitchen is in the front.

'The Robinsons are elderly. He's bedridden and they have a fiercely respectable old housekeeper. Mr Robinson's bedroom overlooks Sundays but not the quarry. His wife spent the evening with him in his bedroom as she always does and went to her own room at nine-thirty. She saw and heard nothing. The housekeeper saw Dunsand come home at twenty to seven and Miss Mowler at eight. She didn't see the Peverils and she herself went to bed at ten.'

Wexford nodded. 'How about Silk?'

'Up in London from June sixth to June eighth, making last-minute festival arrangements. Says he left Sundays at about seven on the evening of the sixth.'

'Can anyone corroborate that?'

'His wife and his two grown-up children are in Italy. They've been there since the end of May and they aren't back yet. Silk says they always go abroad for two months in the summer, but it looks to me as if they aren't as keen as he on the pop scene.'

'And it's his quarry,' said Wexford thoughtfully. 'If anybody had easy access to it, he did. I imagine he's often in

London, too. I don't suppose he was at school with Dawn, was he?'

'Hardly, sir,' said Burden. 'He's as old as you.' He added generously: 'And looks a good deal more.'

Wexford laughed. 'I won't bother to grow my hair, then. It doesn't seem likely that Dawn would have played around with him, and if she had done she'd have gone straight up to the house, surely, not tried to sneak round by a back way. There was no wife at Sundays for her to hide from.'

'And no possible reason for her to bring a picnic.'

'No, I think we can exclude Silk on the grounds of age and general ineligibility. That leaves us with the Peverils, Dunsand and Miss Mowler. But Peveril wasn't alone in his house at five-thirty and Miss Mowler and Dunsand weren't even at home. And yet who but the occupants of one of those three houses could have put Dawn's body in the quarry without being seen?'

Burden glanced surreptitiously at his watch, shifting uneasily. 'Then we're saying she doubled back, sir, and was admitted to one of those houses. Somebody let her in. Not Dunsand or Miss Mowler. Peveril or Mrs Peveril, then? That must mean the Peverils are in it up to their necks. In that case, why does Mrs Peveril say she saw the girl at all? Why say anything?'

'Possibly because she isn't up to her neck in it at all. Because she *did* see Dawn go into those fields and didn't know of any connection between the girl she saw and her husband. Dawn caught that bus because it was the only bus she could catch. She loitered in the fields for two hours—remember how warm and sunny it was—and returned to Peveril's house *after* Mrs Peveril had left for her class. D'you want another drink?'

'Oh, no,' said Burden quickly. 'Good heavens, no.'

'Then we may as well get back to your place. I can't stand this watch-watching.'

Outside the Baptist church the queues had lengthened.

Housewives departing to prepare evening meals had been replaced by working women released from shops and offices.

'Better get something special for the children's dinner,' said conscientious Burden. 'The Luximart stays open late on Fridays. You eating with us?'

'No, thanks. My wife'll have something for me at eight.'

They went into the shop where they were immediately recognised by the manager. He insisted on pointing out to them personally items precisely similar to those Dawn had bought from the six tomatoes in a plastic-covered tray to the bottle of cheap wine. The shop was full and the manager spoke loudly as if anxious to cash in on and reap the benefits of a particularly ghoulish form of advertising.

'Tomatoes as purchased by our very own murder victim,' said Wexford disgustedly.

Burden avoided them studiously and averted his eyes from the row of strawberry mousses. 'You forgot the food in your theory,' he whispered. 'Peveril would have already eaten. His wife would have given him his dinner before she went out.' Regardless of expense, he selected three packages of *bœuf bourguignon* from the frozen-food trough. 'She meant to stay overnight too. You forgot that. Or was Peveril going to hide her in his studio when his wife got home at eleven?'

'Everything all right, sir?' said the manager. 'How about a bottle of wine to go with that?'

'No, thanks.' Burden paid and they left, their progress watched by a dozen pairs of curious eyes. The sun was still bright, the wind brisk. Martin was fixing a fresh, larger, poster of Dawn's picture to the church-hall door.

'Anything yet?' asked Wexford.

'We've had five hundred women pass through here, sir, and not one of them able to give us a bit of help.'

'Keep on at it tomorrow.'

They walked the length of the High Street and turned left into Tabard Road. Burden's step always quickened at this point. Once he had made himself aware that no fire engines or ambulances thronged the street outside his bungalow he relaxed and his breathing became more even.

'Was Peveril going to keep her hidden all night?' he said. 'Or, failing that, maybe she got into Dunsand's place through the larder window. There's an idea for you. Poor old Dunsand who has to fend for himself like me, living on frozen food he buys on his way home, no doubt. Miss Mowler must have actually known her—district nurses know everybody. Perhaps Dawn hid in her garden until eight o'clock, keeping herself from boredom by trying on a dress she found hanging in the shed?'

'I'm the one who asks the derisive questions, not you, remember? All this reversing our roles throws me off balance.' Wexford raised his eyebrows at the three bicycles leaning against the Burdens' gate and the moped parked at the kerb. 'Doesn't look as if your boy's moping in solitude,' he said. 'Good thing he's been prudent and shut the windows.'

The six teenagers who were gyrating energetically in Burden's living room stopped abashed when the policemen came in, and Pat, standing by the record player, pressed the 'reject' lever. Vedast's line, 'Come once more and be my wife', groaned away on a dying fall, the last word a melancholy moan.

'Having your dancing lesson at home tonight, my dear?' said Wexford, smiling.

The two Burden children began to make hasty excuses while their friends made for the door with the silent speed that looks like treachery but is in fact the loyalty of those accustomed to parental censure and who know it is better faced without an audience. Wexford didn't think they ought to have to apologise for innocently enjoying themselves and he interrupted Burden's half-hearted reproaches.

'Play it again, will you, Pat?'

Expertly she found the right track on the L.P. without

having to check with the sleeve and lowered the pick-up arm delicately.

'I don't like you doing that,' said John. 'You'll scratch it.'

'I won't. I'm more careful with records than you are. So there!' The Burden children were usually at loggerheads and seldom missed an opportunity to rile each other. 'It's a horrible song, anyway. All sloppy love stuff. Folk music ought to have some point to it and Zeno Vedast's hasn't any point at all.'

'What d'you mean by "point", Pat?'

'Well, be anti-war, Mr Wexford, or for everybody loving each other not just one stupid girl. Or anti-ugliness and mess like Betti Ho. Zeno Vedast's songs are all for him, all for self.'

Wexford listened interestedly to this but Burden said sourly, 'Everybody loving each other! You can talk.' He sniffed. 'I don't hold with all this putting the world right.'

'Then you shouldn't be a policeman,' said Wexford. 'Play it, Pat.'

The song started with a little grinding scratch which made John frown and purse his lips. Then Vedast's strings twanged and the clear, unaffected voice began to sing:

> 'I don't miss her smile or the flowers,
> I don't eclipse distance or hours . . .'

'He writes his own songs?' Wexford whispered.

'Oh, yes, always,' said John reverently. 'This one's two years old but it's his best.'

'Boring!' Pat ducked behind the player to avoid her brother's wrath.

It wasn't boring. Listening to the slight, delicate story which the verses and the chorus told, Wexford had a strong sense that the singer was relating a true experience.

Suddenly the backing grew loud and Vedast's voice bitter, keening:

'Now she's gone in the harsh light of day,
When she'll return the night would not say,
And I am left to vision the time
When once more she'll come and be mine.

So come by, come nigh,
   come try and tell why
   some sigh, some cry,
   some lie and some di-i-ie.'

Burden broke the silence which followed. 'I'm going to get this food heated up.' He went into the kitchen but Wexford lingered.

'Does he ever write joke songs, John?'

'*Joke* songs?'

'Yes—I mean, well, they're hardly in the same class, but Haydn and Mozart sometimes wrote jokes into their music. If you're a joker in private life, joking often comes into your work as well. D'you know the Surprise Symphony?'

Pat said, 'We did it at school. There's a sort of soft gentle bit and then a big boom that makes you jump.'

Wexford nodded. 'I wondered if Vedast...'

'Some of them are a bit like that,' said John. 'Sudden loud bits or a funny change of key. And all his songs are supposed to be somebody's story or to have a special meaning for a friend.' He added eagerly: 'I'll play you some more, shall I?'

'Not now.' Burden came back to lay the table. Pat tried to take the knives and forks out of his hand, but the daughter who had been admonished for showing insufficient love must not be allowed to show it now by helping her father. He kept his hold on the cutlery and shook his head with rather a martyred air. 'Ready in five minutes. You'd better wash your hands and sit up at the table.'

Wexford followed him into the kitchen.

'I've learnt some interesting facts about our slave-driver. I wonder how long he's staying in this neck of the woods?'

'John says indefinitely. You don't really think he had anything to do with all this?'

Wexford shrugged. 'He intrigues me. I can't do what Scott advises and stop mine ear against the singer. His song is beginning to haunt me. I think I'll buy a single of it tomorrow.'

Burden switched off the oven. 'We might play it over and over in your office,' he said sarcastically. 'Get a couple of the W.P.C.s in and dance. Have ourselves a rave-up. There won't be anything else to do if no one's identified that dress.'

'There will be for me,' said Wexford, taking his leave. 'I'm going to London to have another talk with Joan Miall.'

14

Wexford bought a local paper to read in the train. The *Kingsmarkham Courier* came out on a Friday and Dawn's body had been found on the previous Monday, so that news was stale even by local standards. Harry Wild, the chief reporter, had made what he could of it by giving headline publicity to Wexford's appeals in connection with the red dress, but by far the greater part of the front page was devoted to Zeno Vedast. A large photograph, taken by a not very expert *Courier* staff man, showed the singer and the Tates leaning against the bonnet of the golden Rolls. Nell was smiling serenely, one hand caressing the lion ornament. Wild had married his two lead stories by including in his caption to the picture a frank confession from Vedast that he had been at school with Dawn Stonor. Reading it, Wexford felt even more convinced that Vedast could not be involved in Dawn's death, that he had nothing to hide. But why then was he staying on in Cheriton Forest, staying even though, as the caption stated, he had found and started negotiations for the house he intended to buy? Could it be that he was staying to see the case through, to await the outcome?

Joan Miall's flat was on the second floor of a tall shabby house between the Earls Court Road and Warwick Road. It wasn't a shabby flat, but smartly and even adventurously decorated, the ceilings painted in bold dark colours to reduce their height. A close observer could tell that the furniture was mostly secondhand, but the girls had re-covered the armchairs, put new pictures in old frames and filled the shelves with brightly jacketed paperbacks. There were a great many plants, fresh and green from recent watering.

She received him without pomp, without preparation. She wore red trousers, a red spotted smock and no make-up. A big old vacuum cleaner, cast off perhaps by some more affluent relative, was plugged in just inside the front door. He had heard its whine die away when he rang the bell.

She was expecting him and she put on a kettle to make coffee. 'I miss Dawn,' she said. 'Especially round about lunch-time. We were almost always together then. I keep expecting to hear her call out from her bedroom that she's dying for a cup of coffee. Oh, "dying"—the expressions one uses! But she often said she was dying. Dying of boredom, dying for a drink.'

'I know so little about her. If I knew more, I might know how and why. You see, Miss Miall, there are two kinds of murder victim, those who are killed by a stranger for gain or for some obscure pathological reason, and those who are killed by someone who is not a stranger, someone who might be or have been a friend. It is in those cases that it's invaluable to know as much as may be known about the character and the tastes and the peculiarities of the victim.'

'Yes, I do see. Of course I do.' She paused, frowning. 'But people are little worlds, aren't they? There's so much in everyone, depths and layers, strange countries if we're talking about worlds. I might just be showing you the wrong country.'

It took her a little while to get the coffee. She was a faddist, he remembered. He heard and smelt her grinding coffee beans —nothing pre-ground out of a packet for her—and when she came in with the tray he saw that the coffee was in an earthen-ware jug. But as soon as she sat down she lit a cigarette and she sighed with a kind of relief as she exhaled. It recalled to him her words about the strange countries in each person's make-up. She hadn't mentioned the inconsistencies which

121

those who delve into character must encounter as bafflingly as the unknown.

'Did you both work every night at the Townsman?' he began.

'It's more complicated than that. We do lunches as well. Members can lunch between twelve and three, so we either work an eleven till five shift or one from seven at night to two in the morning. If you do the night shift, you can be sure you won't have to do the lunchtime one next day, but otherwise it's rather haphazard. We get two full days off a week, not necessarily Saturday and Sunday, of course. Dawn and I often worked the same shift, but just as often we didn't. There were lots and lots of times when she was alone here seeing people and getting calls I knew nothing about.'

'You knew about the one particular call you told me of.'

'Yes,' she said, 'I've thought a lot about that since then, trying to sort it all out, and I've remembered all sorts of things I didn't tell you. But the things I've remembered aren't helpful. They really only prove it *wasn't* Zeno Vedast who phoned her.'

'I'd like to hear them just the same.'

'I forgot to tell you that his name came up long before the phone call. It must have been in March or April. Of course, we'd see him on TV or read about him in the papers and she'd say she'd known him for years, but she never actually spoke of him as a friend she *saw*. Then one morning—I think it was the end of March—she said he'd been in the club the night before. I hadn't been working that night and, frankly, I didn't believe her. I knew he wasn't a member. I asked one of the other girls and she said Zeno Vedast had been in and had sort of chatted Dawn up a bit. I still wasn't convinced and I'm not now—about the friendship, I mean. We get a lot of celebrities in the club and they do chat us up. That's what we're there for.'

'When did the phone call come, Miss Miall?'

'It was a Monday.' She frowned, concentrating. 'Dawn had had the day off, I'd been working the lunchtime shift. Let me see—it wasn't the last Monday in May. I think it must have been May twenty-third, about half past eight in the evening. We were sitting in here by ourselves, watching television. The phone rang and Dawn answered it. She said hallo and then something like, "How super of you to phone me." She covered up the mouthpiece and whispered to me to turn down the TV. Then she said, "It's Zeno Vedast." I was embarrassed. I thought she must be in a really neurotic state if she was prepared to fantasise that far.'

Wexford accepted a second cup of coffee. 'Miss Miall, suppose I told you that Vedast did recognise her in the club, that it was he who phoned that night, what would you say to that?'

'That I knew her and you didn't,' the girl said obstinately. 'He was in the club all right. I know that. He talked to her. A maharajah talked to me for half an hour one night but that doesn't make us lifelong friends. I'll tell you why I'm sure it wasn't Zeno Vedast who phoned. When some celebrity really took notice of Dawn—a film star paying her attention at the club, say—she'd be full of it for days. When it was just make-believe—or let-me-believe like in his song—when she saw someone she said she knew in a photograph or on the TV, she'd comment on it, sort of reminisce a bit, and then forget all about it. After that phone call she wasn't a bit elated. She just said, "I told you I knew him," and then she was quite gloomy, the way she was after she'd had a nasty letter from her mother or some man had stood her up.'

'Who did you think had phoned her then?'

'Some new man she'd met,' Joan Miall said firmly. 'Someone who was attracted to her but who wasn't rich enough or well known enough to be worth bragging about.' A shade of sadness crossed her pretty face. 'Dawn was getting a bit old for our kind of work and she didn't wear well. I know that

sounds ridiculous. She was only twenty-eight. But it bothered
her a lot, knowing she'd be past it in a couple of years. She'd
have had to get a different job or—marry Paul. She was
desperate to make everyone believe she was as attractive as
ever and to her way of thinking you measure attractiveness by
the number of successful men who want to take you out.'

Wexford sighed. When you are twenty-five, thirty seems old.
That was all right, that was natural. But surely when you are
forty, thirty ought to seem young? It sickened him that this
girl and her dead friend had moved in a world where to a man
of fifty a girl of twenty-eight was getting 'past it'.

'This new man,' he said, 'you've no foundation for believ-
ing in his existence? Nothing to make you think he existed but
a phone call which I tell you Vedast himself made?'

'Yes, I have. She went out with him the following week.'

'Miss Miall,' Wexford said rather severely, 'you should
have told me of this before. Is this one of the "unhelpful"
things you've remembered?'

'One of the things that prove it wasn't Vedast, yes. But I
don't know his name. I don't even know if he wasn't another
of Dawn's dreams.'

There was a framed photograph on the mantelpiece, an
enlarged snapshot of a dark young man and a girl on a beach
somewhere. Wexford picked up the picture and scrutinised it.

'That's Paul,' said Joan Miall.

It took him a few moments to realise that the girl was
Dawn. In shorts and a shirt, her hair wind-blown, she looked
quite different from the painted, overdressed creature whose
portrait on posters was stuck up all over Kingsmarkham like
a cabaret star's publicity. At last, he thought, she had achieved
a kind of fame. Though posthumously, she had got herself
into the public eye. But she looked happier in the snapshot.
No, happy wasn't the right word—content, rather, tranquil,
and perhaps just a tiny bit bored?

There had been no ecstasy, no excitement, in being on a beach with her ordinary fiancé. Mrs Stonor had seen to that. By belittling her daughter, by comparing her unfavourably to others, by denying her love, she had so warped her personality that everyday affection meant nothing to her. Dawn understood love only when it came from and was directed to money and success, the love of a man who would make her rich and get her name in the papers. Well, some man had got her name in the papers . . .

'Go on, Miss Miall,' said Wexford, laying the photograph down.

'The day I'm going to tell you about was June first. It was a Wednesday and it was Paul's birthday.'

The date meant something to Wexford. He nodded, listening alertly.

'On the Tuesday, the day before, Dawn and I had both had our day off. She went out in the afternoon and bought the blue dress, the one she wore to go and see her mother. I remember I asked her if she'd bought it to take away on holiday with Paul. Well, she said she couldn't make up her mind whether she was going away with Paul or not but she wouldn't say why not, only that it might be boring. They hadn't quarrelled. Paul spent the evening with us and stayed the night with Dawn. They seemed very happy.'

'Let's come to June first.'

'Paul went off to work before we were up. He was going to come back for a birthday lunch Dawn was giving him and then take the afternoon off. Dawn and I were both due to work the evening shift. She went out to buy food for lunch, steak and salad—I insisted on fresh stuff—and after she came back, while she was laying the table, the phone rang. I answered it and a man's voice asked to speak to Dawn. I didn't ask who it was and he didn't say. I gave the phone to Dawn and I didn't stay to hear what she said. I went on with preparing the lunch. She came back into the kitchen and she was very flushed and excited-looking but a bit—well, narked too. I'm explaining this badly but I do remember just what she was like. She was excited and yet she was upset. I could see she didn't want to say who had rung her so I didn't ask.'

'Did you ever find out?'

'No, I didn't. But there's more to come. Paul was expected at half past one. By about a quarter to twelve everything was ready for lunch. We just had to grill the steaks when Paul came. Dawn was already dressed and made-up, but at twelve she went away and changed and when she came out of her bedroom she was wearing her new dress and she'd done her hair on top of her head and put on a lot more eye make-up. In fact, she'd overdone the whole thing and she was wearing far too much perfume. I was sitting in here reading a magazine. She came in and said, "I've got to go out for an hour or so. If Paul gets here before I'm back you can tell him some tale. Say I forgot the wine or something." Well, as I said, we didn't ask each other questions. I wasn't too thrilled about lying to Paul. The wine was already on the table so I couldn't say that. I just hoped she wouldn't be long.'

'Was she?' Wexford asked.

'She went out at sometime between twelve and half past. Paul was a bit late. He got here at twenty to two and still she wasn't back. I told him she had some last-minute shopping, but I could see he was hurt. After all, it was his birthday and they were more or less engaged.'

'When did she come back?'

'Ten past three. I remember the time exactly because when she came in I realised she must have been in a pub and they close at three. She'd had too much to drink, anyway. Her face was all puffy and her speech wasn't quite clear. Paul's a very good-tempered bloke but he was nearly doing his nut by this time.'

'Where did she say she'd been?'

'She said she'd met a girl who used to work in the club and

126

was now a model—poor Dawn could never resist the fame and glamour bit—and they'd gone into a pub and forgotten the time talking.'

'You didn't believe her?'

'Of course I didn't. Later on, after Paul had gone Dawn wrote to her mother to say she'd go and see her on the following Monday.'

'You didn't connect the pub visit with the letter?'

'I didn't at the time,' the girl said thoughtfully, 'but I do now. You see, it was very unlike Dawn to make up her mind about anything to do with her mother on the spur of the moment. She knew she had to go to Kingsmarkham sometimes but usually she'd start sort of arguing with herself about it weeks beforehand. You know, saying she'd have to go but she didn't want to and maybe she could let it ride for a few more weeks. Then she'd write a letter and tear it up and sort of swear about it. It'd take her weeks to get a letter actually written and posted. But it didn't this time. She sat down and dashed it off.'

Wexford said, 'Did she ever mention what happened on June first again?'

She nodded, looking unhappy. 'On the Saturday, the first day of her holiday. She said, "What would you think of a bloke who said he was dying to see you and the best date he could fix up was a few drinks in a pub at lunchtime?" She went to that mirror over there and put her face right close up to it, staring at herself and pulling at the skin under her eyes. "If you were really crazy about a man," she said, "you wouldn't care, would you? You'd just want his company. You wouldn't worry if he was too scared or too mean to take you to a hotel for the night." I didn't really know whether she was referring to me or herself. I thought she might be talking about me because my boy friend is poor. Then Paul came and took her out and I gathered she meant to go away on holiday with him.'

Joan Miall sighed. She reached for a fresh cigarette but the packet was empty. The air in the room was blue with hanging smoke. Wexford thanked her and went away. In the Earls Court Road he went into a record shop and bought a single of 'Let-me-believe'.

15

The red dress was back in Wexford's office. Several thousand women had looked at it, handled it, backed away from the dark stain; not one had recognised it. It lay on the rosewood surface, on the wood whose colour matched it, an old shabby dress, folded, soiled, keeping its secret as implacably as ever.

Wexford touched it, glanced again at the label and at the whitish talc marks around the neckline. Dawn had worn it but she had never owned it. She had found it in Kingsmarkham and for some unfathomable reason had put it on, she who had been fashion-conscious and who was already dressed in garments which matched her shoes and her bag. She had found it in Kingsmarkham, but, unless deception had been practised, no Kingsmarkham or Stowerton woman had ever owned it. A woman never forgets any dress she has owned, not even if fifty years have elapsed between her discarding of it and her being confronted with it again, much less if only seven or eight years have passed.

Burden came into the office, glanced at Wexford, glared at the dress as if to say, Why bother with it? Why let it keep confusing us, holding us up? Aloud he said, 'How did you get on with the Miall girl?'

'It looks as if Dawn had another man friend. Mike, I'm wondering if it could have been Peveril. He was in London on June first, and on that day Dawn met a man for a drink. She went out to meet someone in an underhand way when she had a pretty pressing engagement at home. Now that date took place only five days before the day she died.'

'Go on,' said Burden, interested.

'Dawn was in Kingsmarkham at Easter. The Peverils were already living in The Pathway at Easter. Suppose Peveril picked her up somewhere in Kingsmarkham, had a drink with her, got her to give him her phone number?'

'Didn't he ever phone her?'

'According to Joan Miall, Dawn had a rather mysterious phone call from a man on Monday, May twenty-third. That could have been Peveril. His wife goes out on Monday evenings and that would have given him his opportunity.'

'Sounds promising.'

'Unfortunately, it isn't. We know Zeno Vedast phoned Dawn about that time. He says he did, and Dawn told Joan Miall it was he as soon as she answered the phone. Joan didn't believe her because afterwards she wasn't elated or excited. But, on his own admission, Vedast put her off with vague promises. Dawn wasn't a fool. She could tell he was bored and that rocked her so much that she couldn't even bring herself to brag about knowing him any more or weave any of her usual fantasies. Therefore, I think we must conclude that it was Vedast who phoned her that night and that Vedast had no further communication with her. He's out of it. But that doesn't mean Peveril didn't phone her. He could easily have done so on some occasion when Joan wasn't there.

'During the weekend following her pub date, the weekend preceding her death, she gave Joan to understand that she was embarking on an affair with a man too mean or too scared to take her to an hotel. That description would fit Edward Peveril, a man who owned a house from which his wife would be absent for several hours on a Monday evening; Edward Peveril who came out to us while we were at the festival and tried to distract our attention from the quarry as soon as he knew who we were; Edward Peveril who no longer cares for his wife and who, on Miss Mowler's evidence, is occasionally unfaithful to her.'

Burden pondered. 'What do you think happened that night, then?'

'Whatever happened, Mrs Peveril must know of it.'

'You don't mean connived at it, sir?'

'Not beforehand, certainly. She may have been suspicious beforehand. Don't forget that she told us it was a matter of chance that she was in the house at all at five-thirty. Her *husband* had tried to persuade her to go to a film in Kingsmarkham that afternoon and stay on for her evening class. Why didn't she do that? Because she was suspicious of his motives? Confident that he could persuade her, he asked Dawn to bring with her a meal for the two of them. But Mrs Peveril didn't go out. She saw Dawn at five-thirty, the actual time of the appointment, *and Dawn saw her*. Therefore, carrying her bag of food, she waited in those fields until she saw Margaret Peveril go out.

'Dawn was then admitted by Peveril. She began to prepare the food, changing into an old dress Peveril gave her so as not to spoil the mauve thing. Before the meal was ready, she asked Peveril if it would be all right for her to stay the night as he, knowing this couldn't be but using any inducements to get Dawn to come, had previously promised. When he told her that idea was off, they quarrelled, she threatening to stay and confront his wife. He killed her in a panic.'

Burden said, 'But when Mrs Peveril came home he threw himself on her mercy. She was needed to help him clean up and dispose of the body.'

'I don't know, Mike. I haven't great confidence in this theory. Why did Mrs Peveril mention having seen the girl at all if it's true? I can't get a warrant on this evidence but tomorrow I'm going to ask Peveril's permission to search. Tomorrow's Sunday and it's your day off.'

'Oh, I'll come,' said Burden.

'No. Have your Sunday with the kids. If we find anything I'll let you know at once.'

Wexford allowed his glance to fall once more on the dress, caught now in a ray of evening sunshine which touched it like a stage spotlight. He tried to imagine Margaret Peveril slender, rejuvenated, but he could only see her as she was, bigger and fleshier than Dawn, a woman whose whole build showed that she could never, since her teens, have worn that dress. He shrugged.

He didn't attempt to get a search warrant. With Martin and three constables, he went to The Pathway in the morning, a misty, cool morning such as heralds a fine day. The sunshine hung like a sheet of gold satin under a fine tulle veil.

Muttering and pleading that his work would be disturbed, Peveril agreed without much protest to his house being searched. Wexford was disappointed. He had expected the man to put up a front of aggressive opposition. They lifted the fitted carpets, scrutinised skirting boards, examined the hems of curtains. Mrs Peveril watched them, biting her nails. This ultimate desecration of her home had driven her into a kind of fugue, a total withdrawal into apathy and silence. Her husband sat in his studio, surrounded by men crawling on the floor and peering under cabinets; he doodled on his drawing board, making meaningless sketches which could not, under any circumstances, have been saleable.

Miss Mowler, returning home from church, came up to Wexford at the gate and asked if the men would like tea. Wexford refused. He noticed, not for the first time, how the churchgoing woman who might more conveniently carry a prayer book in her handbag, always holds it ostentatiously in her hands, an outward and visible sign of spiritual superiority. Dunsand was mowing his lawn, emptying the cuttings into a spruce little green wheelbarrow. Wexford went back into the house. Presently he looked out of the window and, to his astonishment, saw Louis Mbowele approaching, his coat swinging open to allow the soft summer air to fan his brown, bead-hung chest. Louis went into Dunsand's garden, the mowing was abandoned and the two men entered the bungalow. Not so very astonishing, after all. Wexford remembered that Louis was a philosophy student at Myringham where Dunsand taught philosophy.

'How are you doing?' he said to Martin.

'She wasn't killed here, sir. Unless it was in the bathroom. I reckon you could stick a pig in that bathroom and not leave a trace.'

'We may as well get out then. This is supposed to be a day of rest and I'm going home.'

'Just one thing, sir. Young Stevens asked me if you'd see him before he goes off duty. He's at the station. He mentioned it last night but what with all this it went out of my head. He's got something on his mind but he won't tell me what.'

The house was restored to order. Wexford apologised sparingly to Mrs Peveril.

'I told you she didn't come here,' she said with a cowed resentful look. 'I told you she went right away from here. She went across the fields.'

Wexford got into the car beside Martin. 'I wish she wouldn't keep saying that, you know, gratuitously, as it were.' He slammed the door. Martin listened politely as he was obliged to do, his mind on his Sunday dinner which would probably be spoilt by now, anyway. 'Why does she say it if it isn't true?' said Wexford.

'Maybe it is true, sir.'

'Then why didn't anyone else see her after five-thirty? Think of all those blokes coming home for their dinners at Sundays and in Stowerton around six. They'd have seen her. She was the kind of girl men notice.'

The mention of dinner made Sergeant Martin even more

obtuse than usual. 'Maybe she sat in the fields for hours, sir, sat there till it was dark.'

'Oh God!' Wexford roared. 'If she was going to have to hang about for hours she'd have stayed at her mother's or if that was unbearable, gone to the pictures in Kingsmarkham.'

'But the last bus, sir?'

'It's less than a mile, man. She was a strong healthy girl. Wouldn't she have walked it later rather than sit about in a field?'

'Then Mrs Peveril never saw her.'

'Oh, yes, she did. She observed her closely, every detail of her appearance.'

The car drew up and the two men got out, Martin to depart for a long and well-deserved dinner, Wexford to see Stevens who was already waiting for him in his office. The shy and inarticulate young policeman stood to attention rigidly which made Wexford even crosser and also made him want to laugh. He told the man to sit down and Stevens did so, less at ease in a chair than stiffly on his feet.

Wexford didn't laugh. He said quite gently, 'We do have a welfare officer, Stevens, if the men have some domestic or private problem that's interfering with their work.'

'But it's work that's interfering with my work, sir,' Stevens stuttered.

'I don't know what you mean.'

The man swallowed. 'Sir.' He stopped. He said it again. 'Sir,' and then, rushing, the words tumbling out, 'Mrs Peveril, sir, I've wanted to tell you for days. I didn't think it was for me to put myself forward. I didn't know what to do.'

'If you know something about Mrs Peveril that I ought to know, you must tell me at once. You know that, Stevens. Now come on, pull yourself together.'

'Sir, I was transferred here from Brighton last year.' He waited for Wexford's nod of encouragement which came with brisk impatience. 'There was a bank robbery, sir, last summer.

Mrs Peveril saw the raid and she—she came to the police voluntarily to give evidence. The superintendent interviewed her a lot, sir, and she had to try to identify the villains. We never caught them.'

'You recognised her? Her name? Her face?'

'Her face, sir, and then when I heard her name I remembered. She knew me too. She was very hysterical, sir, a bad witness, kept saying it was all making her ill. I've had it on my conscience all week and then I kept thinking, well, so what? She didn't hold up the bank clerk. And then it got so I thought—well, I had to tell you, sir.'

'Stevens,' sighed Wexford, 'you've got a lot to learn. Never mind, you've told me at last. Go away and have your dinner. I'll check all this with Brighton.'

He began to have an inkling of what had happened. But he must check before going back to The Pathway. There wasn't going to be any Sunday dinner for him.

The Peverils were just finishing theirs. It struck Wexford that this was the first time he had encountered Peveril not working or coming straight from his work or fidgeting to get back to it.

'What is it this time?' he said, looking up from roast beef and Yorkshire pudding.

'I'm sorry to disturb your lunch, Mr Peveril. I want to talk to your wife.'

Peveril promptly picked up his plate, tucked his napkin into the neck of his sweater and, having paused to grab the mustard pot, was making for the door to his studio.

'Don't leave me, Edward!' said his wife in the thin, high-pitched voice which, if it were louder, would be a scream. 'You never give me any support, you never have done. I shall be ill again. I can't bear being questioned. I'm frightened.'

'You're always bloody frightened. Don't hang on me.' He pushed her away. 'Can't you see I've got a plate in my hand?'

135

'Edward, can't you see, he's going to make me say who did it! He's going to make me pick someone out!'

'Mrs Peveril, sit down. Please sit down. I'd be glad if you wouldn't go away, sir. I don't think it's for me to interfere between husband and wife but, if I may say so, Mrs Peveril might not be quite so frightened if you'd try to give her the support she wants. Please, sir, do as I ask.'

Wexford's tone had been very stern and commanding. It was effective. Bullies crumple fast when sharply admonished, and Peveril, though he moved no closer to his wife and did not look at her, sat down, put his plate on the edge of the table and folded his arms sullenly. Mrs Peveril crept towards him and hesitated, biting her thumbnail. She gave Wexford the half-sly, half-desperate look of the hysteric who is trying to preserve intact the thickly packed layers of neurosis.

'Now will you both listen quietly to what I have to say?' He waited. Neither spoke. 'Mrs Peveril, let me tell you what I think happened. In Brighton you witnessed a bank robbery.' Her eyes opened wide. She gave a little chattering murmur. 'That was a most upsetting experience for you, but you very properly came forward to give information to the police. You were a key witness. Naturally, the police questioned you exhaustively. You fancied yourself badgered and you became frightened, ill perhaps with fright, both from the constant visits of the police and from a notion that some revenge might be taken against you for the information you had given. You moved here to get away from that. Am I right?'

Mrs Peveril said nothing. Her husband, who never missed a cue, said, 'Sure, you're right. Never mind where I had my roots, my contacts, my ideal studio. Madam wanted to run away so we ran away.'

'Please, Mr Peveril.' Wexford turned to the woman, sensing that he must be very careful, very gentle. Her stillness, the compulsive nail biting, the hard set furrows in her face, were ominous. 'You had only been here a few months when you realised, because of what you had seen, that you might soon be involved in another and perhaps even more disturbing criminal case. Mrs Peveril, we know you saw Dawn Stonor on Monday, June sixth. You gave an accurate description of her, more precise than any other we have. I suggest to you— please don't be alarmed—that you either admitted her to this house or saw her enter another house. You told us you saw her cross the fields because you believed that would be the surest way to draw our attention, the attention you find so frightening, away from you and your own neighbourhood.'

It might have been all right. She took her hand from her mouth and bit her lip. She made a little preparatory murmur. It would have been all right if Peveril hadn't started to his feet and shouted at her, 'Christ, is that true? You bloody fool! I thought there was something fishy, I knew it. You told lies to the police and nearly landed me right in it. My God!'

She began to scream. 'I never saw her at all! I never saw her!' A slap on the face would have been effective. Instead, her husband began shaking her so that the screams came out in stifled strangled gasps. She crumpled and fell on the floor. Peveril took a step backwards, white-faced.

'Get Miss Mowler,' snapped Wexford.

By the time he returned with the nurse, Mrs Peveril was lying back in a chair, moaning softly. Miss Mowler gave her a bracing, toothy smile.

'We'll get you to bed, dear, and then I'll make you a nice strong cup of tea.'

Mrs Peveril cringed away from her. 'Go away. I don't want you. I want Edward '

'All right, dear. Just as you like. Edward can get you to bed while I make the tea.'

At the use of his Christian name Peveril frowned ferociously, but he gave an arm to his wife and helped her up the stairs. Miss Mowler bustled about, removing plates of congealing food, boiling a kettle, hunting for aspirins. A little thin woman, she was quick in her movements and efficient. She talked all the time she worked, apologising for non-existent faults. What a pity she hadn't been on the spot when 'it' happened. If only she had been in her garden, for instance. How unfortunate that, what with one thing and another, she had had to wash her hands and take off her overall before accompanying Mr Peveril to the house. Wexford said very little. He was thinking that he would be lucky to get any more out of Mrs Peveril that day.

The tea was taken up. Peveril didn't reappear. Wexford followed Miss Mowler back into her own bungalow where newspapers were spread over the hall carpet and a kind of late spring cleaning seemed to be in progress.

'I spilt a cup of cocoa down the wall. It's a blessing this paper's washable. I don't know what you must think of me, washing walls on a Sunday afternoon.'

'The better the day, the better the deed,' said Wexford politely. 'I want to have another look at the quarry, Miss Mowler. May I make my way there through your garden?'

He was permitted to do so but only after he had refused pressing offers of tea and coffee, sherry, a sandwich. Miss Mowler, having been assured that he didn't need her to accompany him down the path and open the gate for him, returned to her work. He let himself out of the garden and into the narrow no man's land that separated the estate from Sundays.

16

Heavy rains had fallen and now the sun had returned as bright and hot as ever. But it was too soon yet for new grass to show, too soon for even the beginnings of the green carpet which by autumn would once more cover the desert plain which Sundays park had become. Wexford sat down on the edge of the quarry. Here nature was winning, for the flowers and shrubs, the delicate yet lush herbage of June, had been assailed by only half a dozen trampling feet. New roses, new harebells, were opening to replace the crushed blossoms. He looked at the broken wire, the wall, the three gates, but they told him nothing more, and gradually the scented air, sun-warmed and soft, drove thoughts of the case from his mind. A butterfly, a Clouded Yellow, drifted languidly past him and alighted on a rose, its petals paler and creamier than the buttercup-coloured wings. Not so many butterflies these days as when he was a child, not so many as when even his daughters were children. Under his breath he caught himself humming a tune. At first he thought it was that song of Vedast's which stuck in his mind and irritated him. Then he realised it wasn't that one but a ballad of Betti Ho's in which she prophesied that her children would never see a butterfly except in a museum. The Clouded Yellow took to the air again, hovering, floating . . .

'You're trespassing!'

Wexford started to his feet, shaking himself out of his dream.

'You're trespassing,' said Silk again, half-serious, half-peevishly ironic. 'I don't see why I should always have the fuzz trampling over my land.'

Looking up into the irritable white face and the smiling black one, Wexford said, 'I'm not trampling. I was sitting and thinking. What are you two up to? Planning another festival?'

'No, we're going to try and get a commune going here during the university vacation. Louis and I and his girl friend and about half a dozen others. Louis wants to see how it works out with a view to operating a kibbutz system in Marumi.'

'Really?' said Wexford blankly. He didn't see how gathering together a house party in a fully-equipped and furnished mansion could be a rehearsal for kibbutzim in an equatorial state, but he didn't say so. 'Well, I think I'll trample off now.'

'So will I,' said Louis unexpectedly. He gave his radiant grin and patted Silk on the grey head which reached just to his shoulder. 'Peace be with you.'

They skirted the Peverils' fence and emerged at the head of The Pathway. Mrs Peveril's bedroom curtains were drawn. Dunsand was pulling puny little weeds out of his flowerless borders. Beside Miss Mowler's car a bucket of soapy water stood unattended. It was hot, sunny, a radiant day. The English do not relax in deck-chairs in their front gardens and, apart from the crouching figure of the philosophy lecturer, the place was deserted. Louis waved graciously to him.

'Want a lift into Kingsmarkham?'

'Thanks,' Louis said. 'That way I might get the three-thirty bus to Myringham.'

Wexford's car was a fair-sized one, but no car except perhaps Vedast's Rolls would have been roomy enough to accommodate Louis Mbowele comfortably. Laughing, he hunched himself inside the folds of his pony-skin and slid the passenger seat back to its fullest extent.

Wexford said, 'When you get to the top of wherever it is you're going, are you going to *make* them live in communes?'

'It's the only way of life, man.'

'And force them to be equal and dictate the pattern of their houses and the subjects of their study and operate a censorship and forbid other political parties?'

'For a time, for a time. It's necessary. They have to learn. When they see it all works and the new generation's grown up and we have peace and full bellies, then we can start to relax. It's necessary to make them do what they aren't just too crazy to do right now. So you have to make them for their own good.'

'Do you know a saying of James Boswell? "We have no right to make people happy against their will"?'

Louis nodded, smiling no longer.

'I know it, man, and I know the connection in which it was said. The slave trade. The traders excused themselves on the ground that my people would be happier on plantations than in jungles. This is different. This is for real. And it's only for a time.'

'Oh, Louis,' said Wexford, turning into the Forby road, 'that's what they all say.'

They drove into Kingsmarkham in silence. The heat of the day, his failure to get anywhere, enervated Wexford. There seemed nothing else to do with his afternoon but go home, eat his stale lunch, maybe sleep. Then, as they approached the place where the Myringham bus stopped, he became aware of the long silence and wondered if he had offended the young African. Louis looked as if he would have a hearty appetite, and the Olive and Dove did a good Sunday lunch. . . .

'Have you eaten?' he said.

'Sure. I cadged some bread and cheese off Len.'

'Mr Dunsand? Why did you have to cadge? Isn't he very hospitable?'

Louis grinned. Evidently, he hadn't been offended, only sleepy from the sun. 'He's a recluse, he said. 'He finds it hard to communicate. Still, I took him out to lunch a while back in

Myringham—last Wednesday fortnight it was—so I guess he owed me a meal. I asked him to join our commune but he's not together enough for that.'

'Strange. You'd think a lecturer in philosophy would . . .'

'Have found the way? Found himself?' Louis leapt out of the car and strode round to open Wexford's door. 'That's a popular misconception, man. It's living—a broad spectrum of living—that teaches you how to live, not philosophy. Philosophy teaches you how to *think*.'

The bus was late. Louis, scorning to join the queue, sat down on the steps of the Snowdrop Cleaners, and Wexford, leaving the car at the kerb, followed him.

'How do you get on with him?'

Louis considered. The dozen or so people in the queue bestowed upon him glances of intense, if repressed, curiosity. Few black-skinned men and women had penetrated to this country town, and to them his coat, his beads and the green silk scarf he wore round his head—although no more than fashionable 'gear' for black and white alike—perhaps appeared as tribal paraphernalia. He returned their looks with the gracious smile of a prince, a tawny Rasselas, and said to Wexford:

'He's all right as a teacher, he knows his subject. But he doesn't seem to like people. You see, he's afraid of them.'

'What else is there to be afraid of?' asked Wexford to whom this idea, in all its truth, had come suddenly as if out of the air. 'Except, maybe, thunderstorms, floods, what insurance companies call Acts of God. If you say you're afraid of bombs or war, it's people who make the bombs and the war.'

'You're right. But, oh, man, there are a lot of people and they are frightening. And it's worse when one of the people you're frightened of is yourself.' Louis gazed into the heart of the afternoon sun. 'Someone told me he was better when his wife lived with him. He used to go away on holidays then, the Majorca bit, the Costa Brava scramble. He doesn't do anything now but read and paint the house and mow the lawn. But you can't picture him married to *her*, can you?' Louis got up, thrust out his hand. 'Here's the bus.'

'Picture her? I don't know her. Do you?'

Extending one huge furry arm to support her, Louis helped a fragile-looking old lady on to the bus platform. In the manner of one whose girlhood dreams have at last been realised and who has fallen into the hands of a sheikh, she blushed, giggled and almost panicked. The other passengers stared and whispered.

'Come along now,' said the driver. 'We haven't got all day.'

Louis grinned. Head and shoulders above the rest, he gave his fare, looking over a diminutive woman's hat at Wexford.

'I don't know her. Old Silk told me who she was at the festival, pointed her out while Zeno Vedast was singing. Man, you stood next to her.'

'I did?'

The bus started.

'Peace be with you,' Louis shouted.

'And with you,' said Wexford.

The golden car wasn't there. Perhaps it had been silly of him to think it would be. On such a fine afternoon they would all have gone out to see the house Vedast was buying. On the almost bare forecourt, blanched ashen pale by hard sunlight, his own car looked forlorn. The Cheriton Forest Hotel seemed asleep. But the porter who had admired Nell Tate was awake. He sat in the deserted hall, reading the *Sunday Express* and smoking a cigarette which he stubbed out quickly when Wexford appeared.

'I'm afraid not, sir,' he said in answer to the chief inspector's enquiry. 'Mr Vedast and Mrs Tate went out in Mr Vedast's car after lunch.'

'You don't know when they'll be back?'

Memories of fifty-pence pieces easily earned stirred in the

porter's mind. He was obviously reluctant to deny Wexford anything. 'Mr Tate took his coffee out into the garden, sir. Would you care for me to ... ?'

'No, I'll find him myself.'

'As you like sir,' said the man, philosophically contemplating the smaller coin his efforts had won him.

Wexford strolled round the gabled, studded, mullioned and heavily rose-hung building. There was nobody about. Birds sang sleepily in the deciduous trees which bordered the fir plantations. He reached the back and saw the elderly couple with whom he had shared the Shakespeare Lounge snoring in long chairs on the terrace. A gravel path wound between rose-beds to a small round lawn in the middle of which was an umbrella with a table and chair under it. A man sat in the chair, his back to the terrace. The porter, a tactful servant, had described Tate as taking his coffee in the garden and there was certainly a diminutive cup on the table beside him. But what Tate was taking was brandy. An eager hand had just grasped the bottle of Courvoisier and was about to tip a further measure into the already half-full glass.

'Good afternoon, Mr Tate.'

If Wexford had hoped to make Tate jump he was disappointed. The man didn't get up. He filled his glass, replaced the bottle top and said, 'Hallo. Have a drink.'

Wexford remembered that he was driving, that he had had no lunch, and he refused. 'I'd like to talk to you. D'you mind if I fetch myself a chair?'

'No,' said Tate economically.

Wexford fetched himself a deck-chair and drew it under the umbrella's shade. Tate didn't say anything. His face quite blank, he contemplated the view of the hilly forest, lying black and furry-looking, and a smooth blue sky. He wasn't in the least drunk. Alcoholics never get drunk. Wexford thought that this was probably Tate's misfortune, that he had drunk so much and drunk so chronically that, perpetually intoxicated, he could never now enjoy the felicity of what most people call intoxication. His skin was a rough greyish red, his eyeballs veined with red, their rims vermilion and moist. And yet he was a young man still, unlined, thin, not bad-looking, his hair untouched by grey.

'Mr Tate, I really wanted to talk to your wife.'

'She's gone out with Zeno to see the new house.'

As he had thought. 'So Mr Vedast found one to his liking?'

Tate agreed that this was so. He sipped his brandy. 'It's called Cheriton Hall.'

'Ah, yes. I think I know it. On the Pomfret side of the forest. Will you all live there?'

'We go where Zeno goes.'

Guessing, hoping, very much in the dark, Wexford essayed, 'Your wife won't find it awkward living so comparatively close to her ex-husband?'

The unhealthy colour in Tate's face deepened, the grey overpowering the red. He made no answer but he fixed on Wexford a truculent and rather puzzled stare.

'I'm right in thinking your wife was once married to Mr Dunsand?' Tate shrugged. The shrug implied an indifference to Wexford's opinions rather than a doubt as to their veracity. 'For the past week,' Wexford went on, 'I've been trying to discover a connection between Dawn Stonor and some resident of the Sundays estate, especially of The Pathway. Until now I've been unable to succeed.'

'Small world,' said Tate uneasily.

'Is it? I think it's an enormous world. I think it's extraordinary that Dawn should have last been seen alive in The Pathway where Mrs Tate's ex-husband lives. I think it particularly odd now that I know Dawn was once a close friend of Zeno Vedast who is now a—er, close friend of your wife's. And yet I'm to dismiss it as being due to the smallness of the world.'

Tate shrugged again. 'Zeno and Nell and me were all in

145

Duvette Gardens that night you're talking about.' He put Vedast's name before his wife's, Wexford noticed. 'We were all together and that guy Silk looked in about ten to talk about the festival.' Morosely, he said, 'We've never been near that place.'

'Surely you were when you were at the festival, very near? Didn't your wife point Mr Dunsand's house out to you?'

It was a trap and the slow-witted Tate fell into it. 'She said, that's Len's house, yes.'

Wexford pounced. 'So she knew it? He'd only lived there a matter of weeks but she knew it. Not by the street name and the number. She knew it by the look of it!'

'I shouldn't like to have your job, meddling in people's private affairs.'

'And I shouldn't like to have yours, Mr Tate,' said Wexford crisply. He leant across the table, forcing the other man to look at him. 'Whose wife is she, yours or that singer you fawn on? Yours or the man who divorced her? What sort of a set-up are you running here? Or do you do just what you're told, lie, pimp, connive at obstructing the police, anything he and she tell you?'

There was too little of one kind of spirit in Tate and too much of the other for him to react violently to these insults. He passed a hand across bleary eyes as if his head ached and said in a sour cowed voice, 'Christ, how you do go on! Never you mind my wife. I can deal with her.'

'By blacking her eye?'

'She told you? I bet she didn't tell you why.'

'I think it was because you found out she'd been seeing Dunsand. At the festival when she pointed out his house you put two and two together. You didn't mind about Vedast, that was different. Maybe you found she'd got a key to his house so you had it out with her and blacked her eye.'

Tate half-smiled. It was the smile of one who is accustomed to subservience to a superior intellect, a smile of grudging

146

admiration. He took something out of his trouser pocket and laid it on the table. A key.

'I found it in her handbag. It'll be safer with you. She might get it away from me and use it again.' He got up abruptly, took his bottle and walked very carefully and steadily up the terrace steps and into the hotel.

Wexford pocketed the key. He tiptoed past the old couple, made his way through a cool and shadowy corridor to the front entrance. Then, seeing the golden car had arrived, he slipped back into the porch and waited.

Nell and Zeno Vedast got out. The swelling had gone down from the girl's eye and her painted face was almost serene. Her hair, freshly washed, was a yellow cloud but the bright light showed darker roots. Vedast, wearing jeans and a thin embroidered waistcoat, took a springy stride towards Wexford's car and stood contemplating it, smiling, his head on one side. His face wore very much the expression Wexford had seen there just before Tate drank the doctored liquor, and he heard him say:

'That parking ticket we got, shall we put it on his windscreen?'

'What's the point?' said Nell.

'Fun is the point, Nello darling. A joke. He'll twig it in two seconds but think how mad he'll be first. Go and get it, Nello. It's on the back seat.'

She opened the rear door of the Rolls. Hypnotised by him, obedient as ever, she gave him the ticket. But as he was lifting one of the wipers she broke out:

'I'm sick of jokes. Why can't we grow up, do things for real? I hate always playing games.'

'Do you really, Nello? You are a funny girl.' Vedast clipped the ticket under the wiper and laughed. He shook back his hair and his yellow eyes glowed. 'I don't believe you. I think you liked all that funny dressing up and pretending to be good and making cosy little plans.' He took her hand,

147

kissed her cheek lightly. 'That's why we get on so well, dear, you and me with our little fantasies. Shall we go and rouse Goffo from his Sunday stupor?'

She nodded, clutching his arm. They went off towards the rose garden. When they had disappeared around the side of the hotel Wexford emerged thoughtfully. Having a strong objection to the scattering of litter, he placed the parking ticket under the paws of the golden lion and then he drove away.

17

Some little good had come out of Mrs Peveril's hysterical breakdown. The information she was now willing to give was imparted too late to be of much use—Wexford knew it already, or most of it—but her despair had shocked her husband into anxiety for her.

He said soberly, 'You were pretty decent, very patient actually. I never realised what a bad state she'd got herself into. Will she have to appear in court?'

'I don't know, Mr Peveril. I still don't quite know what she did see. I must have a final word with her.'

'If she does have to I'll be there. She won't mind so much if I'm with her. The fact is I've been too wrapped up in my work. I let her face all that business in Brighton alone and it was too much for her. When this is over I'm going to scrape up the cash and take her away for a good holiday.'

The uxoriousness wouldn't last, Wexford knew that. Such a *volte-face* often takes place at crises in a marriage but it is only in romances that it becomes a permanency.

And Peveril revealed just how ephemeral it was when, as they went upstairs to see his wife, he muttered, 'You have to bloody wet-nurse some women all their lives, don't you? If I'm not wanted for the next half-hour I may as well catch up on a spot of work.'

Mrs Peveril, wan-looking but calm, sat up in bed wrapped in a jaded broderie anglais dressing gown.

'It was like you said,' she admitted. 'I wanted to make you all think she'd gone a long, long way from here. I wanted to

149

be left in peace. When I first saw her I meant to tell Edward what I'd seen but I didn't because he gets cross with me if I gossip. He says he works for me all day and all I've got to do with myself is look out of the window and tell stories about the neighbours.' She sighed heavily. 'Then when Mrs Clarke phoned me on that Sunday night and said you were coming round asking, I thought I'd say she'd gone into the fields. If I'd said she'd gone next door you'd never have left me alone. I thought saying I hadn't seen her at all would be perjury.'

Wexford shook his head. It was quite useless to point out to her that what she had said was equally perjury.

'You saw her go next door to Mr Dunsand's? At what time?'

'At half past five. I did say,' said Mrs Peveril, eagerly attempting to retrieve her integrity, 'I saw her at five-thirty. I watched her. I saw her go into the porch and someone must have let her in because she never came out again.' Prevarication at an end now, Mrs Peveril was cheerfully burning her boats, gabbling out belated information. Wexford knew she was speaking the truth. 'I was very interested. You see, I couldn't think who she could be. Mr Dunsand never has any visitors except sometimes his students.'

'Never?' Wexford asked quickly.

She said ingenuously, 'Oh, no, I should have noticed. I spend a lot of time at my window when Edward's in his studio and you can see everything these light evenings, can't you? That's why I was so *intrigued* by this girl.' Fear touched her afresh and the wan look returned. 'You'll protect me, won't you? I mean, when I've been to the court and said how Mr Dunsand did it you won't let me come to any harm?'

'When you have been to the court and told the truth, Mrs Peveril,' Wexford corrected her, 'we'll see that you're quite safe.'

With a passing, thoughtful glance at Dunsand's bungalow,

its windows closed against the midsummer evening, Wexford drove to Tabard Road. He found Burden and the children in the garden and for once there was no music playing. Burden was too respectable and had far too much social conscience to allow record players or transistors out of doors. The boy and girl sat at a wicker table, arguing and making some pretence of doing their homework. John, who was always pleased to see the chief inspector whom he regarded as an ally and friend of oppressed youth, fetched him a chair and said:

'Could you give me a bit of help, Mr Wexford? I've got to do an essay on the French Revolution, and Dad's no use. He's not educated.'

'Really!' spluttered Burden. 'Don't be so rude.'

His son ignored him. 'I've left my book at school and I can't remember the new names the Convention gave to the months. I'll have to know them and I thought . . .'

'I'll try.' Wexford hesitated. 'We're in *Messidor* now, that's June. You're supposed to start with September. Let's see . . . *Vendemiaire, Brumaire, Frimaire; Nivose, Pluviose, Ventose;* then *Germinal* like Zola's book, *Floreal* and *Prairial; Messidor, Thermidor* and—wait . . .'

'*Fructidor!*' exclaimed John.

Wexford chuckled. 'You might care to know the contemporary and rather scathing English translation: Wheezy, Sneezy, Freezy; Slippy, Drippy, Nippy; Showery, Flowery, Bowery; Wheaty, Heaty, Sweety. There, you can put that in your essay and maybe you'll get an A.' He cut short the boy's thanks and said, 'One good turn deserves another. Now I want a bit of help from you.'

'Me?'

'Mm-hm. About Zeno Vedast. Or, more precisely, about Godfrey Tate. You must know something about him. You told your father who his wife was.'

'I read about it,' John said, 'in the *Musical Express*. Anything about Zeno's news, you see.' He put down his pen and

151

flashed a look of triumph at his father. 'What d'you want to know, Mr Wexford?'

'Anything about Zeno. What you read.'

'Zeno ran her over in his car ...'

'He *what* ... ?'

'It was like this. He went to Myringham to give a concert—it was sponsored by that Mr Silk, Silk Enterprises—and there was a big crowd outside the theatre afterwards and she got in front of his car and got hurt. It said in the paper that Silk Enterprises paid for a private room in the hospital for her and sent her flowers and fruit and things. I expect Zeno thought that would be good publicity, don't you? It was about two years ago, maybe three. Dad,' said John resentfully, 'won't let me save copies of old magazines. He says it's hoarding. She was married to someone else then. I think he was called Dunn, something like Dunn.'

'Go on.'

'When she got married again it was in the papers because Zeno was at the wedding and Mr Silk. I expect she'd rather have married Zeno.'

'I daresay she would, John, but he wouldn't have her so she took the next best thing. Catch as catch can.'

'Good heavens,' said Burden crossly, 'must you fill him up with these cynical views of life?'

Wexford winked indiscreetly at the boy and for the time being said no more. He was thinking of the bald story he had been told and, more particularly, of the gaps in it which only an older person with experience of life could fill. Nell was still young. She must have been very young when she first married Dunsand. He wondered what had led to that ill-assorted marriage, what had made her choose the reserved, repressed lecturer for a husband. An unhappy home life like Dawn Stonor's? The need to escape from some dreary backwater? If this were so, it must have been a case of out of the frying pan into the fire. He pictured her among the faculty wives, decades her senior, the long evenings at home with Dunsand; the leather chairs, Wittgenstein, the lawn-mowing . . . Still a teenager at heart, she must have longed for younger people, for music, for excitement. And yet there was in her the stuff that makes a slave. Had she also been Dunsand's slave? Perhaps. But she had escaped—into a glamorous, eventful, luxurious life that was nonetheless slavery. About two years ago, at the time the song was written.

> 'So come by, come nigh,
>   come try and tell why
>   some sigh, some cry,
>   some lie and some die.'

He had sung it aloud and the others were staring at him. Pat giggled.

John said, 'Very groovey, Mr Wexford.'

In the same parlance Wexford said, 'I shouldn't make much bread that way, John. Apart from not being able to sing, I don't have the figure for it.' He raised his heavy body out of the chair and said rather sharply to the inspector, 'Come into the house.'

'First thing tomorrow,' Wexford said, 'I want you to swear out a warrant to search Dunsand's house.'

'What, another fruitless search?'

'Maybe it won't be fruitless.'

Burden took Pat's ballet shoes off the seat of one chair and John's tennis racket off another. 'On what evidence, for God's sake?'

'If Mrs Peveril has any value as a witness at all, Dawn Stonor went to Dunsand's house. She was last seen going to his house and she was never seen coming out of it, never seen again. I would calculate that it's a shorter distance from his back fence to the quarry than from any other back fence. She was killed in that house, Mike.'

'Will you ask Dunsand's consent first?'

'Yes, but he'll refuse. At least, I think so. I shall also ask him not to go to work tomorrow. They come down this week, so he can't have anything very pressing to do.'

Burden looked bewildered. 'You were just as sure it happened in Peveril's house, sir. Are you saying she knew Dunsand, that it was Dunsand she met in that pub on June first?'

'No. I know it wasn't. Dunsand was in Myringham on June first. Louis Mbowele told me that.'

'And Dunsand can't have let her in on that Monday. He wasn't there at five-thirty. We're as certain as can be she didn't know Dunsand. Can you imagine him picking a girl up, asking her to come to his house?'

'You must remember that Dunsand isn't the only person who could have let her in. Nell Tate had a key.'

'She used to go and see her ex-husband?' Burden asked doubtfully.

'I should think not,' Wexford rejoined slowly. 'Mrs Peveril would have seen her if she had been and Mrs Peveril never saw her. Perhaps he sent her the key in the hope that she would visit him. The fact remains that she had a key and she could have been in Dunsand's house by five-thirty. Did you ever check on that Duvette Gardens alibi?'

Burden looked a little offended. He was conscientious, proud of his thoroughness. 'Of course I did. Although, there didn't seem much point when you got so interested in Peveril. I got the Met. on it.'

'And?'

'Vedast's car was stuck outside all day and all night, gathering his usual parking tickets. Nobody seems to have a clue whether they were inside the house. One of them may not have been. We just can't tell.'

Wexford nodded. 'The Tates would lie themselves black in the face to protect their master and he'd lie to protect his little ones. I think he cares a good deal more for "Goffo" than for "Nello", though, don't you? I wish I could see a motive. One might suggest that Nell was jealous of Dawn's relationship with Zeno Vedast, only there wasn't a relationship any more. Vedast might have had a date to meet Dawn somewhere in the neighbourhood and Nell found out about it and lured her into the house to kill her. D'you fancy that idea?'

'Of course I don't.'

'Tate might have fallen in love with Dawn when they met at the Townsman Club and got the key from his wife to use Dunsand's house for a love nest. Then Vedast killed her to prevent her spoiling their jolly little *tria juncta in uno*. Does that suit you better?'

'Well, I suppose anything's possible with people of their sort.'

'Sure it is. Nell arranged to meet Dawn there because she had Dunsand's loneliness on her conscience. She thought Dawn might make him a suitable second wife—no less suitable than his first, at any rate—but when Dawn had confessed that Vedast had phoned her, shown interest in her, Nell got into a rage. She would, of course, have instructed Dawn to bring with her a second-hand red dress because Dunsand likes second-hand clothes, red is his favourite colour, and he prefers dresses to be a tight fit.'

Burden said distantly, 'I don't see the point of all this, sir. Aren't you rather arguing with yourself? It's you who want to search the place, not I.'

'I expect I am, Mike,' said Wexford. 'I haven't an idea how it happened, but two things I'm certain of. We shall find traces of blood in Dunsand's house tomorrow, and Dunsand will confess to having killed Dawn Stonor from the chivalrous motive of protecting his former and still much-loved wife. It's going to be a heavy day so I think I'll be off home now.'

18

While they ransacked the bungalow, Wexford sat with Dunsand in the sombre living room. The search warrant had been shown to him and he had read it carefully, scrupulously, in total silence. He lifted his shoulders, nodded and followed Wexford into the living room, pausing at the window to pick a dead flower off one of the dehydrated cacti. Then he sat down and began to leaf through one of the travel brochures in the manner of a patient in a doctor's waiting room. The light fell on his glasses, turning them into gleaming opaque ovals. His eyes were invisible, his thick mouth closed and set, so that his whole face was expressionless. But as he turned the pages and came to one on which some words had been pencilled in the margin, there came suddenly a tightening of those rubbery cheek muscles that was like a wince.

'Your wife had a key to this house, Mr Dunsand.'

He looked up. 'Yes. I sent it to her. But she's my wife no longer.'

'I beg your pardon. We believe she or a friend of hers was here on June sixth.'

'No,' he said. 'Oh, no.'

Wexford thought he had closed his eyes, although he could not be sure. He was aware of a terrible stillness in the room, a profound silence, which the movements in the hall and overhead accentuated rather than disturbed. Dunsand was not in the least like Godfrey Tate to look at or in manner, yet they shared this strange reticence. Both Nell Tate's husbands possessed the rare quality of being able to answer a searching question with a straight yes or no. Had she chosen them for this or had she made them so? Had she chosen them at all? The man Wexford could be sure she had chosen was chatty, verbose, an extrovert whom some would call charming.

He tried again. 'Do you ever see your former wife?'

'No.'

'Never, Mr Dunsand?'

'Not now. I shall never see her again now.'

'You're aware that she's staying at the Cheriton Forest Hotel?'

'Yes. I saw it in the paper, a picture of her with a lot of flowers. She used to fill the house with flowers.' He glanced at the moribund cacti and then he picked up his brochure again. Underneath it on the pile was a pamphlet advertising dishwashers and another for garden equipment. 'I'd rather not talk any more now, if you don't mind.' He added curiously, 'I'm not obliged to say anything, am I?'

Wexford left him and went into one of the bedrooms. Bryant, Gates and Loring were crawling about, examining the carpet.

'Are there any women's clothes in the wardrobes?'

'No, sir, and there's no blood. We've done the whole place. This is the last room. We've even been up in the loft.'

'I heard you. Contents of the refrigerator?'

'It's empty. He's been defrosting it. He's very houseproud, sir. If you're thinking of that food she bought, the dustbins have been emptied twice since June sixth.'

Aghast, suddenly weary, Wexford said, 'I *know* she was killed here!'

'The hall floor's bitumastic, sir, the kind of stuff that's poured on as liquid and then left to set. There are no joins. I suppose we could get it taken up. We could have the tiles off the bathroom walls.'

Wexford went back into the room where Dunsand was. He

cleared his throat and then found he was at a loss for words. His eyes met not Dunsand's own but the thick baffling glass which shielded them. Dunsand got up and handed him two identical keys.

'One of these,' he said in a calm, neutral voice, 'is mine. The other I sent to my former wife and she returned it to me by post.' Wexford looked at the keys, the first of which was scraped and scarred from daily use, the second scarcely marked. 'Mrs Tate,' said Dunsand with awful precision, 'was never here. I should like to make a point of that.' Things were happening, Wexford thought, at least to some extent according to the pattern he had forecast. Dunsand swallowed, looked down at the floor. 'I found the girl here when I got home on June sixth. She must have got in by a window. The kitchen fanlight had been left unfastened. I encountered her as soon as I let myself in. She was giving the place what I think thieves call a "going over". We struggled and I—killed her. I hit her with a bottle of wine she had left on the hall table.'

'Mr Dunsand . . .' Wexford began almost despairingly.

'No, wait. Let me finish. She had brought some things with her, apart from the wine, some shopping in a bag and some clothes. Perhaps she thought my house was empty and she meant to camp there—"squat" is the word, isn't it? After it got dark I put her body in the quarry and the other things into the river under the bridge. Then I washed the floor and the walls.' Staring at Wexford, he said abruptly, 'Aren't you going to caution me? Shouldn't there be witnesses to take all this down?'

'This confession—you insist on making it?'

'Of course. It's true. I killed her. I knew it was only a matter of time before you arrested me.' He took off his glasses and rubbed them against his sleeve. His naked eyes were frightening. There was something terrible yet indefinable in their depths, a light that told perhaps of passion, of single-minded fanaticism under that flaccid exterior. He was used to teaching, to instructing. Now, in a teacher's voice, he proceeded to direct Wexford.

'The proper thing, I think, will be for me to go to the police station and make a statement.' He put on his glasses, wiped a beading of sweat from above his left eyebrow. 'I could go in my own car or accompany you if you think that wiser. I'm quite ready.'

'Well, you were right,' said Burden in grudging admiration.

'Only up to a point. We didn't find a trace of blood.'

'He must be a nut or a saint, taking that on himself to shield a woman like Nell Tate.' Burden began to pace the office, growing vehement. 'That statement he made, it doesn't even remotely fit the facts. For one thing, Dawn was let into the house. She didn't go round the back. And for another, why should she suppose Dunsand's house to have been empty—I mean, unoccupied? If she had, she wouldn't have camped there on her own. She had a home to go to. Can you see Dunsand beating a woman to death because he suspected her of breaking into his house? Crocker said her killer was mad with rage, in a frenzy. That phlegmatic character in a frenzy?'

'He and Tate,' said Wexford, 'are apparently both phlegmatic characters. They are still waters which not only run deep but which may have turbulent undercurrents. Strange, isn't it? Dunsand hasn't asked for a lawyer, hasn't put up the least resistance. He's behaved almost fatalistically. That woman breaks the men she doesn't want but can't scratch the surface of the man she does want.'

Burden shook his head impatiently. 'What do we do now? What next?'

'Go back to Dunsand's place, I suppose. Have another look round and experiment with those keys a bit.'

Bright noon in The Pathway, the hottest day yet of a summer that promised to be all halcyon. The sun had brought into blossom tiny pink flowers on the plants in Miss Mowler's garden. In the meadows in the crook of the arm-shaped road they were cutting hay, cropping flowers far more lush and vigorous than those man had planted. The crude pink of Dunsand's bungalow was blanched to a rosy pallor by the hard hot light.

Wexford went up to the front door and tried Dunsand's keys. Both worked. The third key, the one Tate had given him, looked different, and by now he was sure it wouldn't move the lock. It didn't.

'It's a much older key than the others,' said Burden. 'What's Tate playing at?'

'Let's go inside.'

The whole house had been searched, but for evidence of a crime, not for clues to a life. Wexford remembered how Dunsand had planned to redecorate the place. He held on to that, certain it must have some significance. In a week's time perhaps that ugly wallpaper, those wriggling black stems, those golden flowers, would have been removed. Dunsand would have stripped it down, replaced it. But Dunsand had confessed...

Reticently, disliking the job, he went into the living room where the cacti were, where Dunsand had sat, blindly studying his brochures, and opened the desk. He found no letters, only bills; no marriage certificate, no album of photographs. But in a small drawer under the roll-top he discovered Dunsand's address book, a brown leather-covered book very sparing of entries. A London phone number was recorded under the letter T, just a number followed by a dash and the name Helen. Wexford noted the code and thought it might probably be Vedast's. He looked under S and under D but found no reference to Dawn Stonor.

It was at this point that it occurred to him how she, the dead, she whose death was the cause of this enquiry, had for some days past seemed to fade from its screen. It was as if she, as a real person, a personality, had lost her importance, and that he was searching for the answer to some other puzzle in the ramifications of which her death had been almost incidental. And he saw her—vividly but briefly—as a pawn, a used creature, her life blundering across other, brighter lives, falling through folly and vanity into death.

But the vision went, leaving him no wiser, and he thrust his hands once more into the pigeon-holes of the desk. A bunch of photographs came to light at last. They were in an envelope stuffed into a slot at the side of the roll-top interior, and they were mostly snapshots of Dunsand, much younger, with people who were evidently his parents, but underneath them were two much larger shots which Wexford took to the window. The strong light showed him first a wedding photograph, Dunsand still young, Dunsand smiling down without reserve at his bride in her badly fitting wedding dress, her veil wind-blown, young bony hands clutching a tight posy of rosebuds. Unless he had been twice married, the bride must be Nell. Time and art had changed her so much in the intervening years—eight? Ten?—since the picture was taken as to make her scarcely recognisable as its subject. Her hair was dark, cropped short, her face fresh and childlike. But it was she. The big yearning eyes were unchanged and the short upper lip, showing even in those days its petulant curl.

He brought out the other photograph, the last one, from under it. Nell again, Nell fractionally older, her hair still short and feathery, her skin apparently innocent of make-up. The portrait was coloured, tinted in the shades of old china, rose and sepia and ice-blue and plum red. Nell's new wedding ring gleamed brassily against the dull red stuff of her dress, and on the simple bodice, just below the round neckline, hung a pearl drop on a gold chain.

Wexford went ponderously out into the hall.

19

On all-fours Burden was examining the floor and the hideous shiny wallpaper with its pattern of little gold flowers and tiny, regularly recurring crimson leaves, wallpaper which met a floor that curved up to join it without any intervening skirting board.

'Get up, Mike. It's useless. We've done all that already.'

'One must do something,' said Burden irritably. He got up and brushed his hands against each other. 'What's the matter? You've found something!'

'This.'

'It's the dress! But who's the girl?'

'Nell Tate.'

Burden stared incredulously at the portrait. Then he put it beside the wedding picture, nodded, looked up at the chief inspector. 'I like her better how she was,' he said quietly.

'So would most men, but maybe she doesn't know that.' Wexford slipped the two photographs back into the envelope. 'Mike, I've a curious feeling I'm losing touch with Dawn Stonor, that she's fading away from me and I'm coming to grips with something stranger, something almost more terrible than her actual death. There must be many murder victims,' he said slowly, 'who meet their deaths without knowing in the least why they are to die.'

'Most of them, I should think. Victims of poisoners, old shopkeepers who know the till's empty, all children.'

'She wasn't a child,' said Wexford. 'Perhaps your list isn't

162

completely comprehensive. I don't know, Mike. I'm only dreaming, not really getting anywhere. This is a gloomy place, isn't it? The windows are huge and yet the light doesn't seem to get in. Of course, it's an illusion, it's something to do with the dulling, deadening influence of the man's personality.'

They moved back into the living room where the books frowned on the blue birds and the orange lilies that covered the walls.

Burden said, 'We're getting too dreamlike for me. I'd be happier if I could understand about the keys, if I could see how Dawn got in here.'

'Someone let her in. Someone asked her to come and that someone was here to let her in when she arrived at five-thirty. Not Dunsand.'

'But he cleared up the mess. He was left to dispose of the body he found when he got home.'

'I suppose so. You talk about mess, Mike. What mess? Where is it? Where are the traces of it? Is this killer the one killer we've ever come across who can commit a crime as bloody as this one and leave no blood? I don't believe it.'

'This place will have to be taken apart,' Burden said, crossing the passage and entering the bathroom. 'If it was done without leaving any apparent trace it must have been done in here.' He looked at the gleaming taps, the spotless bath and basin. The sunlight showed no film of dust on glass, no fingermarks on mirrors.

Wexford nodded. 'Yes,' he said, 'the tiles off, the pipes out. And if that yields nothing, the same with the kitchen.'

'Dunsand may crack. He may tell us what at the moment he's doing his utmost to conceal.'

'If he has anything to conceal.'

'Come on, sir. He must know more than he's told us. He must know why his wife would kill an unknown girl in his house, how it happened, the circumstances. He must know that.'

'I wonder?' said Wexford. 'Does he know any more than that his wife—the woman he still thinks of as his wife—may be in danger? I believe he knows very little, Mike, as little of the whole of it as the girl who died.'

Wexford stared up at the ceiling, scanned the smooth glossy walls. The whole place smelt soapy, too clean.

'Mind you don't trip,' said Burden. 'Your shoelace is undone. It's no good looking up there. It's no use looking at all. If she was killed here, someone worked a miracle of butchery.'

Wexford stooped down to re-tie the lace. A bright circle of gold, a little sunbeam refracted through a pane, had lighted on the wall beside his left leg. He stared at the trembling illumination. The gold flowers occurred on the paper in vertical lines about two inches apart, a thin black stripe dividing each line from the next, and the red leaves, pear-shaped, were printed in clusters of three between each flower. Flower, cluster, flower, followed each other immaculately and evenly to meet the bitumastic ridge. There were signs of faint blurring on the pattern, the result perhaps of washing the paper, but nothing had been obliterated. Three leaves, flower, three leaves . . .

'Mike,' he said in a strange voice, 'your sight's better than mine. Have a look at this.'

'I looked before and you stopped me. It's been washed. So what?'

'You were looking for signs of washing, maybe for a missing bit of the pattern. Look again.'

Impatiently Burden got to his knees. He concentrated on the puddle of light.

'Not a missing leaf,' said Wexford. 'In the lowest cluster there aren't three leaves but four.'

They squatted down side by side and examined the hall paper.

'You see,' Wexford said excitedly, 'in this one and this one, in all of them, there are three little pear-shaped leaves like the leaves in a fleur-de-lis. But in the one we're looking at there's a fourth leaf under the centre one.'

'And it's not quite the same colour. It's darker, it's browner.'

'It's blood,' said Wexford, and he added wonderingly, 'One little spot of blood.'

'Shall I ... ?'

'No, don't touch it. The experts can come here, get their sample themselves. It's too precious for us to mess about with. Mike, d'you realise that's the one real piece of evidence we've got?'

'If it's blood, if it's hers.'

'I know it's hers. It has to be.'

They went outside where the sun blazed on the road, melting tar and creating, where concrete ended and fields began, a mirage like a veil of shimmering water. The car was oven-hot inside, its seats burning to the touch. Burden rolled down his window and drove in his shirt sleeves.

'Now to check the key,' said Wexford.

'Which one, sir? The one that didn't fit?'

'Yes. I think we'll find a door that it will open.' Sweating profusely, Wexford pulled down the eyeshade across the windscreen. 'But that's a simple job, a job for Martin.'

'I'm not with you,' said Burden, falling into line behind the bus that, with its load of Sundays estate passengers, made its way along the sunny road to Kingsmarkham. 'I haven't a clue what particular door you expect it to unlock.'

Wexford smiled. 'A lot of doors are beginning to unlock inside my head, Mike, but this one, this actual door, is in Myringham. It's the door to the house Dunsand lived in before he moved here.'

The afternoon wore on and the heat seemed to mount, reaching the eighties by four o'clock. Wexford shut himself up in his office, the windows open, the blinds down. He sat alone, waiting, thinking, and then, on the principle that it is better to shut away a problem whose answer continually eludes one, to exclude it and return to it later, he resumed work on that crime-prevention directive which had lain unattended since before the festival.

The reports began to come in. The blood was human and of Dawn Stonor's group. The key which Tate had given him in the hotel garden opened the door of Leonard Dunsand's former home in Myringham. But at Sundays, where questioning of housewives had continued all the afternoon, no one had been found to say that she had ever seen Nell Tate, much less observed her call at Dunsand's house.

The five-twelve bus stopped outside the Baptist church. Wexford watched the passengers get on it. A girl came out of the Luximart, carrying a brown paper bag. She wasn't wearing mauve, she wasn't in the least like Dawn, and she was going to her new house at Sundays, not to her death. Wexford phoned the Cheriton Forest Hotel. Yes, Mr Vedast was still there. Mr Vedast planned to leave that evening. The receptionist couldn't say any more, perhaps, if Wexford was the press, she had said too much already . . .

He turned the sheets of the crime-prevention directive face downwards. He returned to his problem as the day began to cool and the sun's rays slanted. At seven he went across the road to the Carousel café where he found Burden and his children eating steak and salad while Emmanuel Ellerman's hit song 'High Tide' brayed at them from wall speakers.

'Pity you've eaten,' said Wexford. 'I was going to take you out to dinner at the Cheriton Forest.' He ordered a sandwich. 'We shall have to be content to take our coffee with Zeno Vedast instead.'

'I don't suppose . . .' began John wistfully.

'I'm afraid you can't come, John. This is a serious visit, an official visit.'

'Pat and I were going to hang about in the High Street to see him pass through. He's going back to London tonight.'

'I don't think he'll be going just yet,' said Wexford.

20

The receptionist put a call through to the Elizabethan Suite. 'Mr Vedast says will you wait, please? Mr Vedast is engaged at present.' She was young, the right age to be among Vedast's adorers. 'If you'd care to go into the Shakespeare Lounge, it's over there on the ...'

'We know the way,' said Wexford.

There was no one in the lounge but the dog. It got up when they came in, stared at them morosely, then collapsed again some two yards from where it had previously been lying.

'I'm in the dark,' said Burden, impatiently rejecting the magazines Wexford passed to him. 'I think you ought to tell me why we're here.'

'Why are we ever anywhere?' Wexford sighed. 'To ask, to deduce, to conclude and to catch. Only it's a little different this time.'

'Oh, riddles, philosophy. What I want to know is . . .'

'Wait.'

Godfrey Tate had come very quietly into the room, Godfrey Tate in his usual dapper black that made his torso look as thin as a teenager's and his limbs spidery.

'Zeno's got that guy Silk with him,' he said, without greeting, without preamble. 'He says to ask you what you want.'

Wexford said quietly, 'I want to tell him what I think of him.'

Tate was bemused with drink, not 'high' on alcohol, but low, dulled, cut off, almost somnambulistic. 'Do I tell him that?'

'Mr Tate, it's a matter of indifference to me what you tell him. Why is Silk here?'

'He'd heard Dunsand's been arrested. He came to tell Nell.'

'And now you're celebrating?'

Tate blinked at him. He turned, shuffled towards the door.

'See you,' said Wexford, looking at his watch, 'in ten minutes.'

But before the ten minutes were up—minutes in which Burden had picked up magazine after magazine, discarding them all, and Wexford had sat still, watching the hall—Martin Silk emerged from the lift. Long hair on the elderly makes its wearer look like a nineteenth-century statesman, but in Silk's case the resemblance ended at his neck. He wore a white tee-shirt with a bunch of grapes appliqued on the chest. As he passed the reception desk he swaggered like a proud adolescent, thrusting his hips forward, but as he neared the lounge door he began to scuttle, an old man getting away from trouble.

'Mr Silk!'

Silk stopped and forced a broad smile, creasing his face into a thousand wrinkles, enclosing his eyes in cracked parchment skin.

'I hope we haven't driven you away,' said Wexford. 'You're welcome to stay as far as we're concerned.'

Sidling into the lounge, Silk perched himself on the arm of a chair. His knee joint cracked as he swung one leg.

'Merely a social call,' he said. 'I dropped by to tell Zeno there's quite a crowd waiting in Kingsmarkham to give him a send-off. Of course,' he added spuriously, 'I shall be seeing a lot of him now he's bought this lush pad.'

'But you've always seen a lot of him, haven't you, Mr Silk? One might say that you've been a sort of . . .' Wexford glanced meaningly at the shaggy grey hair, '. . . a sort of *éminence grise* in his life. Or are you another slave?'

'I don't know what you mean.'

'But for you he'd still be Harold Goodbody and he never would have met Nell Dunsand.'

Silk stared at him. 'I acted for the best. We can't know what tragedies may hang on our small actions. I gave to youth a musical genius. If Dunsand freaked out, if certain people were—well, expendable...'

'Is that how you see it? Mr Silk, you interfere too much. You organise too much. Be warned, and don't interfere with Louis Mbowele. You might cause a war this time.'

'Really, I think you're twisted, sick. You're not together. Who is, at your age?' He sneered. 'The hung-up generation.'

'If I belong to it,' Wexford retorted, 'so do you. We're the same age. Only I know it, I accept it. You don't. I accept that all the sport is stale and all the wheels run down. And when I consider what some people call sport, I'm not all that sorry.'

At Wexford's words, particularly the reminder of his true age, a look of real pain crossed Silk's face. Mirrors show us what we want to see, but sometimes we look into living, human mirrors and then, briefly, the fantasising has to stop. Wexford was fat, Silk skinny, the one in a crumpled old suit, the other in tee-shirt and jeans, but they were both sixty. The mirror comparison lay in their shared age, the shared weariness of muscle and bone, and painfully Silk saw it.

He said shrilly, 'What are you doing here?'

'Talking to you at the moment. Now we're going upstairs to talk to your genius.'

'But you've got Dunsand. Zeno wasn't even there. I was with Zeno and the Tates in Kensington. You've got Dunsand under lock and key!'

'What an old-fashioned expression!' Wexford mocked. 'Can't you find a more trendy way of putting it? Come on, Mike, we've wasted enough time.'

They walked up. Silk stood at the foot of the staircase watching them, hesitating, torn perhaps between a fear of his protégé coming to harm and an even greater fear of more cruel jibes levelled at him concerning his age.

Wexford said, 'He knows nothing about it. He knows less even than Dunsand.' He smiled obscurely, tapped on the door of the Elizabethan Suite.

They were packing. At last they were going home. His face an even duskier red than usual, Tate was on his knees, trying to fasten an overfull suitcase, while Vedast sat cross-legged on top of a lacquer cabinet watching him. Wordlessly, Nell led them through the labyrinth of piled luggage and mountains of frippery, magazines and records.

Dead flowers, smelling foetid, were heaped on the balcony. Fresh flowers had arrived that day, perhaps that afternoon, roses, lilies, carnations, and they were dying too. No one had bothered to put them in water.

Nell was as carefully dressed and made-up as usual, but her exertions in the heat had given her an air of dishevelment, for it was still hot, the evening air windless, the sun a smouldering crimson knot over the forest. She scowled at the policemen, met Vedast's cool gaze, and turned immediately to look at herself in one of the mirrors. Vedast gave a light laugh.

'Fasten that case, Goffo. Get a move on, dears. Why don't you go and order some coffee, Nello?' He swayed his body towards Wexford. 'That will give her a chance to repair her poor face,' he said as if she wasn't there.

Burden, who had followed the chief inspector's example and cleared a seat for himself, said gruffly, 'No coffee for us.'

'Just as you like.' Vedast flicked his fingers at Nell, who, still in front of the mirror, was apathetically fidgeting with her hair while watching the policemen in the glass. She sprang round as if those snapping fingers had actually touched her, fetched his orange juice and handed it to him with a pleading look. He removed a lump of ice and licked it. 'How glum you all look!' he said, surveying the four faces. 'You're frightening my little ones, Chief Inspector. Why don't we take it as read. I know what happened and so, presumably, do you —now. It *did* take you a long time. But you can't prove it. So why don't we just congratulate each other like clever cats and mice and you pop off home?'

Wexford quoted softly, ' "What need we fear who knows it when none can call our power to account?" '

The Tates looked at him uncomprehendingly, Nell edging closer to Vedast, who said, 'Macbeth. I sometimes think of changing over to the legitimate theatre. I've had no end of offers.' He swallowed what remained of his ice cube. 'But I don't want to start now, thank you so much. We're none of us feeling quite strong enough for drama.'

'You mean you've had enough of it? You've made your tragedy and now you're exhausted? The function of tragedy, as I'm sure you know, Mr Vedast, is to purge with pity and terror, and that's what I'm going to try to do to you—or some of you. So sit down, Mr Tate, and you too, Mrs Tate, and listen to me.'

Both Nell and her husband looked doubtfully at Vedast for instructions. He nodded lightly.

'Do what the man says, dears.'

Nell flounced on to the sofa, tipping off a heap of dirty clothes and what seemed to be a stack of fan letters. A full glass in his hand, a hand which trembled, Tate crept towards her.

She made a slight movement of rejection, turning her shoulder and at the same time spreading out her thick, stiffly embroidered skirts so that there was no room for her husband to sit beside her. He gave her a bitter look, a look of dark reproach, from under swollen veined eyelids. Clasping his drink as if it were a protective talisman, he perched himself on the sofa arm.

The singer watched them, amused that they had obeyed so easily. A law unto himself, he got down from the cabinet and lounged against the open french window. With the setting of the sun, a light breeze had begun to blow. It fanned his hair, lifting it into a golden aureole. Outside the blue of the sky was deepening to violet, feathered with flamingo red. The frosty orange glass glowed in his hand like a lamp. He stood as if he were about to sing. his chin lifted, his hips thrust forward, quite still, utterly relaxed.

'A tragedy,' said Wexford, 'in two parts.'

'It concerns,' he began, 'two people who by their looks and the power of their personalities were able to command obsessive love. You, Mr Vedast, and you, Mrs Tate. I'm not flattering you. Anyone may become the object of such love and, in my experience, those who do are usually shallow, narcissistic and self-centred.'

Nell said shrilly, 'Are you going to let him talk to me like that, Godfrey?'

Hunched up, nursing his glass, Tate gave her a black look. He said nothing. The breeze chilled him; making the dark hairs on his wrists stand erect.

'The need to love like this lies in the characters of the lovers who fasten generally on the first desirable person who comes in their way, fasten and, if they can; hold on. Unfortunately, the beloved objects trade on this and use it for their own ends, for cruelty and victimisation. Just in case Mrs Tate is under any misapprehension as to whom I mean when I speak of the man who loves her obsessively, in case she should be so obtuse as to suppose I mean Mr Vedast, I'll tell her now that I refer to her first husband, Leonard Dunsand. A foolish, clever, learned, dull and conventional little man who has loved her since she was eighteen when he married her.'

One of those people who will bear any insult provided it carries with it a hint of flattery, Nell apparently couldn't resist preening herself at this. She crossed her long and very shapely legs and gave a sidelong glance in Vedast's direction.

Vedast stroked the string of beads he wore, running them through his fingers.

Wexford went on: 'Who is probably the only man sufficiently capable of self-delusion to love her sincerely, the only man who ever will.' He waited for some reaction from Nell's present husband. Tate reacted characteristically, behaving as he always did in crises or threatened crises. Without getting up, he reached for the brandy bottle. 'If you are in a position to be thankful for anything, Mr Tate, be thankful that you are more sophisticated and have eyes to see. Pity you've clouded them so much with that stuff.'

'I can look after myself,' said Tate in a low voice.

'I never saw a man less capable of doing so, unless it is Mr Dunsand.'

'I'll look after Goffo.' Vedast turned idly, smiling, cooling his hands on the glass, caressing it. 'Do tell us who's in love with me. I'm dying to know.'

'Thousands, I imagine. The one in particular I speak of is dead. She was dying for you too often and at last she really died. You were her first lover. That's supposed to have some profound effect on a woman and, whether it's true or not, it had a profound effect on Dawn Stonor. I wonder how much of that story Mr and Mrs Tate know?' While Vedast resumed his scanning of the sky in which a few pale stars had appeared, Wexford leant towards the Tates. 'They were at school together, Dawn and a boy called Harold Goodbody, a boy who went to tea with his girl friend's grandmother because he only had baked beans at home; Harold Goodbody who wore his cousin's cast-off shoes and whose father spent the housekeeping on dog racing; Harold Goodbody who played April Fool tricks to amuse his friends, who doubtless carried young Dawn's satchel for her. A rustic idyll, wasn't it? Dawn Stonor and her first love, Harold Goodbody.'

'I would prefer you not to call me that,' said Vedast, and for the first time Wexford heard an edge of temper to his voice.

'You'd prefer me to go away, but I shan't do that,' Wexford flashed back. 'You said you were dying to hear and you shall hear.' He leaned back, pleased at the unease his words had provoked in Nell, pleased by Tate's cringing. 'You left your friend,' he said to Vedast, 'and went to London. For you the idyll was over. Soon afterwards she went to London too, but by then you were beyond her reach. And yet she never forgot you. She told her friends and she pretended, perhaps to herself as well as to her friends, that you had always remained lovers and between you was some enduring bond.' Wexford glanced at Burden and inclined his head, giving the inspector honour for this idea which at first he had ridiculed. 'In fact,' he went on, 'nearly a decade passed by before you saw each other again. In that time you had become very famous, many exciting things had happened to you. Very little had happened to her. She was a waitress in a club and she remained a waitress.

'It was a pity you ever went into that club. If you hadn't, Dawn might at this moment be making wedding plans with her fiancé. Why did you go?'

Vedast shrugged. 'This bloke asked us. We hadn't anything better to do.'

'You could hardly have done worse.'

'I didn't kill her. I never touched her.'

Wexford turned towards the Tates, to Godfrey Tate whose bloodshot eyes were wide open and staring.

21

'I shall now go back,' said the chief inspector, 'to one of your exciting happenings, although I don't believe you'll regard it as a highspot when you come to write your memoirs. I refer to your meeting with Mrs Tate, and to describe that I must return to the other love story.'

A glance from Vedast was enough to make Nell get up and switch on the rose-shaded lamps. She moved stiffly, tripping over the red grip and cursing. Vedast gave her his empty glass and she refilled it. He took it without thanks like a duke receiving the drink he has ordered from a parlourmaid.

'Ice, Nello,' he said.

She spooned two cubes out of a pool of water in a bowl on the cabinet. Tate was crouched over his brandy, gazing into the golden liquid. The rosy light played on him, muting the harsh blackness of his hair. Nell gave Vedast his glass again, keeping her hands clasped round it so that his fingers would brush hers as he took it. They brushed them as a stranger's might without lingering. She seemed desperate to stay beside him, to remain with him on the cool, darkening balcony whose rail, reddened by the setting sun, was now a black filagree trellis behind the mound of dead blossoms.

'Go away, Nello. You fidget me.'

She hung her head, crept just inside the window and dropped on to an upright chair, her arms hanging limply by her sides.

'That's right, Mrs Tate, sit where I can see you. You're a very good-looking woman, but you've changed a good deal since you were a bride for the first time. For one thing, you've tinted your hair. I don't suppose you ever wear dark red these days, do you?

'Mr Dunsand liked your short dark hair. He liked you in simple, wifely dresses. I understand from what information was gathered today in Myringham that you were known as a quiet little thing, a good cook, fond of flowers, of home-making, but inclined to be bored with the society you moved in. They were all so much older than you, those faculty wives, weren't they? You would have preferred the company of your husband's students. Those coffee mornings, those empty after-noons, were very dull for you. But they were nothing to the evenings when, after you had prepared the kind of meal Mr Dunsand liked, you had to sit for hours alone with him, the record player switched off, and plan together your annual holiday, plan your budget, decide what new equipment or furniture you could afford that year.

'To Mr Dunsand it was the very essence of contentment. I expect you played your part well. Women like you, born sycophants, usually do, and all the time they wait quietly for the means of escape. Your chance came when Zeno Vedast, your idol, gave a concert in Myringham. I don't suppose Mr Dunsand wanted you to go to that concert. The idea of his wife, the wife who depended on him utterly for her support, disporting herself among a bunch of teenagers at a pop con-cert, can hardly have appealed to him. No, he couldn't have liked to think of you raving among his own students, but you went. If you hadn't gone, Dawn Stonor would be alive today, making wedding plans with her fiancé.

'I don't think you threw yourself under Mr Vedast's car deliberately—you wouldn't have the courage—let's say it was an unconscious urge you couldn't control or resist.

'Mr Vedast had put you in a private room at the hospital. How you must have prayed for Mr Vedast himself to appear with the grapes and the chocolates! You didn't know him.

177

You don't know him now. He sent his minion, and it was any port in a storm for you, Mrs Tate. But you're not unique, don't think it. Many a master in the past has married a likely wench off to his servant so that he can have the enjoying of her without any of the trouble.'

'You've no right to insult me!' Nell flared. She waited for her husband to defend her. When he said nothing, while Vedast smiled and sipped his orange juice, she said, 'Why shouldn't I have left my husband? Why shouldn't I have got married again? I'm not the only one. I was sick to death of living with Len.'

Vedast turned. He said smoothly, 'Like the judges say, this isn't a court of morals, Mr Wexford.'

'Oh, but it is. It must be because it can't be a court of justice.'

'In that case . . .' Nell got up. 'In that case, I'm going. Let's go, Zeno. He can't keep us here.'

'Do as you like, Nello.' Vedast gave her a sly sidelong glance. She couldn't do as she liked. She never had been able to. 'You go if you want,' he said in the voice, usual with him, that was both gentle and unkind. 'I'm staying. I'm fascinated. How about you, Goffo, are you going to take your wife away or stay and support your old mate?'

'Mr Tate stays,' said Burden sharply.

Wexford just glanced at him, raising his eyebrows. 'Let us have an intermission,' he said. 'An interval to relax in. If my voice were better, I'd offer to sing you a song, but in this company . . .' He hesitated, then said, 'You all know the song. It was written at the time of Mrs Tate's second marriage. It would be ingenuous of me to suppose it doesn't illustrate a true story, render someone's real suffering. That's why it was written. Poets,' he said, 'are said to make little songs out of their great sorrows. You . . .' His eyes went to the window, '. . . amused yourself and feathered your luxurious nest by making a song out of someone else's'

178

Vedast jerked round. He came into the room, his yellow eyes sharp and narrow.

'I'll sing it,' he said. 'There's nothing wrong with my voice.'

Wexford nodded. He could tell what Burden was thinking, that his son, that any fan at the festival, would have given a week's wages, a month's grant, a term's pocket money, to have been in their shoes. Vedast, who could command thousands for one concert, was going to sing in private for them. He felt a little sick.

In the pale rosy light, the soft kind light, Vedast looked very young, a teenager himself. He stood in a corner of the room, resting his bare elbows on a shelf from which rose-buds hung, young, fresh rose-buds dead before they opened from dehydration. He waited in the silence of the evening, the silence of the forest which surrounded them. The first word came loud like a note vibrating from a string, then the clear, light voice dropped a little, filling the room with sweet bitterness.

Nell watched the singer adoringly, tapping in time to the tune throughout the first verse, the first chorus. Wexford frowned at her and she tossed her head, flinging herself back petulantly against a cushion. His sickness was passing. He listened to the words as if he had never heard them before, as if he had never fully understood the depth of their meaning.

> 'Remember me and my life-without-life,
> Come once more to be my wife,
> Come today before I grieve,
> Enter the web of let-me-believe.
>
> So come by, come nigh,
>   come try and tell why
>   some sigh, some cry,
>   some lie and some die ...'

179

There was no applause. Vedast dropped his head. Then he flung it back, shaking his hair.

'Thank you,' said Wexford crisply. 'It's all in that song, isn't it? All Mr Dunsand's sorrow is there. He pleaded with you, I imagine, not to break with him entirely, not to leave him utterly without life, to let him believe sometimes, very occasionally, that you were still his wife. And you repeated these conversations to Mr Vedast, giving him such a good idea for a song.'

Tate looked up, frowning, a trickle of brandy coursing down his chin. He wiped his mouth on his sleeve.

'Why did you agree to what Mr Dunsand asked?'

'I didn't want to hurt him too much,' Nell muttered.

A dull, humourless laugh escaped from Burden and it was echoed, surprisingly, by Tate. Wexford didn't laugh. 'Mrs Tate, is that you talking? *You?* When have you ever minded whom you hurt, you who are an expert treader on other people's dreams? If you won't tell me why, I shall have to guess.'

'It was to nark me,' Tate interrupted.

'But you didn't know until after the festival,' Wexford said quickly.

Bewildered, Tate said, 'That's true. She'd been seeing him two or three times a year, going to his house and bloody well sleeping with him. I blacked her eye for her.'

'So you told me. And you gave me a key. Only it wasn't the key to Mr Dunsand's house in The Pathway. It opens the front door of his former home in Myringham. Mrs Tate had never been to The Pathway house. She knew it only because Mr Dunsand described it to her over the phone as the middle house of the three. But he sent her a key, intending that she should keep up the custom of the Myringham days.'

Tate said slowly:

'What custom? What are you on about.'

'I believe you, Mr Tate, when you say you knew nothing of

these visits of your wife's until after the festival when, frightened of what she had done but not frightened enough to confess everything, she told you she had been seeing her first husband. I believe you are entirely innocent of this crime, in no way an accessory. You had been kept in the dark as you are, I daresay, about many things.' Tate shrugged awkwardly. The level of golden liquor in the bottle was going steadily down. He poured himself some more in silence. 'Nor do I think you would have been a party to any of this had you known about it,' said Wexford.

'Mr Vedast wasn't in the dark. He knew. Mrs Tate told him she had promised these—shall I say loans?—loans of herself to Mr Dunsand. And so I come back to why. Why did she do it? You're not a very happy woman, are you, Mrs Tate? Apparently you have everything you wanted, but only apparently. I think that very soon after your second marriage you saw what you had got, luxury and excitement, yes, but at what a price. Another not very inspiring husband—forgive me, Mr Tate—though a complaisant one, a condescending master, kind when you were obedient. So you agreed to Mr Dunsand's request for the sake of the contrast. Those few evenings, those nights, you spent with him, showed you that what you had was at least preferable to your former married life. After a night in Myringham you could go back to London, to Europe, to Bermuda, your loins girded, as it were, with the memory of the alternative.'

'Is that true, Nello? I never knew that.'

'I'm glad to be able to tell you something you don't know, Mr Vedast. But you knew of the part she played while she was there, didn't you? I'm sure Mrs Tate told you all the details, the props, the costume required, shall I say? I'm sure she told you of the setting of the little play they enacted two or three times a year, the activities, following always the same pattern, in which the actors indulged, marriage *à la mode*

Dunsand. Indeed, I know she did. Had she not, you wouldn't have been able to play your—your practical joke.'

Nell said, 'I want a drink, Godfrey.'

'Get it yourself.'

She did so, clattering the bottle neck against the glass, spilling vermouth on to the pale embroidery on her white linen skirt. It made a red stain like blood.

Wexford said, 'I expect you thought all this very amusing, Mr Vedast, until there was a threat of the performance of this play interfering with your own plans. About a month ago Mrs Tate told you that she would be paying her first visit to Mr Dunsand's new home on the afternoon of Monday, June sixth. But that didn't suit you, for you and Mr and Mrs Tate would only just have returned from Manchester where you had a concert engagement.'

Tate shook his head. 'No, that's not right,' he said. 'He meant to stay over till the Monday. It was me said at the last moment it'd be too tiring for him.'

'Ah.' Wexford sighed. 'Even better—or worse. When Mrs Tate first confided in you, you intended that she and you and Mr Tate would all be away from the South on June sixth.' He looked at Nell, at the red stain on her dress which she had not attempted to remove, at the red colour that burned her face. 'Why didn't you just change the date of your appointment with your first husband, Mrs Tate? Surely you could have put it off for a few days?'

For a moment she looked as if she were searching in her mind for an excuse. She put out a trembling hand to Vedast who ignored her, who smiled, his head on one side.

'Because that would have "hurt" Mr Dunsand?' Wexford went on relentlessly. 'Or did you do what you always do, obeyed Mr Vedast?'

In a small, thin voice, she said, 'I left it to Zeno.'

'You left it to Zeno. He was to get in touch with Mr Dunsand, was he? He, a world-famous singer, a pop idol, was to

182

phone Mr Dunsand and tell him you couldn't make it but would, say, Wednesday do instead?'

She was near to tears. She held her hands crushed together so that the peeling nails dug into the flesh. 'You know it wasn't like that. You know you're just tormenting me.'

'Not everyone is as zealous as you, Mrs Tate, about the feelings of others. Not everyone is as anxious as you to go through life without doing hurt. But it's true that I know what happened.' Wexford got up and walked over to Vedast who had taken up a Yoga position, a half-Lotus, on the floor by the open window. He stood over the singer, looking down, his own grey eyes meeting the amber ones.

'No, Mr Vedast,' he said. 'To a person of your temperament it was far more amusing to keep the date, changing not the day but the female protagonist.'

Tate broke the silence.

'What d'you mean? I don't follow you. Female whatsit, what does it mean?'

Wexford came over to him. He spoke gently. 'It means, Mr Tate, that your employer saw a way of getting Mrs Tate out of her appointment, and perhaps all further similar appointments, and at the same time of playing one of his favourite jokes.

'He decided to send a substitute for your wife to The Pathway. First, I suspect, he thought of sending a call girl. But why go to all that trouble when he could send Dawn Stonor whose acquaintance he had renewed some weeks before and whom he had telephoned on May twenty-third?'

22

Wexford sat down in the centre of the room. 'I don't know why you phoned Dawn last night,' he went on, addressing himself directly to Vedast. 'I think your motive was akin to Mrs Tate's motive for visiting her former husband. Probably at the Townsman Club you contrasted Dawn's humble situation with your successful one, remembering how you came from similar beginnings, how you had had even chances of money, fame, glory—but you had achieved them and she had not.

'On May twenty-third Mr and Mrs Tate were away. You were bored. Perhaps you even felt insecure. Why not phone Dawn, do a little slumming, so that afterwards you might have the pleasure of appreciating what you are and what you might have been? I daresay that phone conversation had the desired effect on you. You were quickly tired of her eagerness and you rang off, having vaguely suggested you see each other "sometime" but not, in fact, ever intending to see her again.

'During that week, I believe, Mrs Tate told you of the visit she planned to make to Mr Dunsand's new house. On the phone you had already, I think, boasted to Dawn of the house you were yourself thinking of buying near Kingsmarkham. Why not play a joke, the biggest joke of your career?'

'My thought processes,' said Vedast, 'don't work quite like that. Stop hovering, Nello. Go and sit down somewhere.'

The only spot in the room where she wanted to be was at his side. She looked at the sofa where her husband sat hunched, at the two occupied chairs, at the empty chairs which were either near her husband or near the policemen. And like an insect with bright antennae, bright wings, she fluttered desperately, hovered, as Vedast had put it, finally alighting—her heels were high, her shoes platformed—on another spot of carpet as near to him as she had been when he had shooed her away. The insect had come back to the flame.

Wexford had paused when the interruption came but, apart from hesitating briefly, he took no notice of her.

'The first of June,' he said to Vedast, 'was the birthday of the man Dawn was very probably going to marry, the man she would have married if you had left her alone. She was at home, waiting for him to come to lunch. You didn't know that. Would you have cared if you had? You phoned her in the morning and asked her to meet you for a drink.' Burden stirred in his chair, his eyebrows lifting. 'She wasn't very elated about it. Perhaps she realised that a man like you, a man as rich as you are, who could afford without noticing it the most expensive restaurant in London, only takes a girl for drinks in a pub if he despises her, if he thinks she isn't worth any more. But she dressed carefully for you just the same; changing out of the clothes that were good enough for an ordinary fiancé.

'And later, when the excitement of that lunchtime date had begun to recede, she asked herself—and her flatmate—if she *was* despised, if that was the reason why you were only prepared to have a hole-in-corner, *sub rosa* affair with her, hiding her in a house no one knew you had bought instead of taking her to an hotel.

'In that pub, between one o'clock and three, you asked her, after some preliminary flattery and flirtation, no doubt, to spend the night of the following Monday with you in your new house. Of course, she agreed. She would be on holiday. She could go and see her mother and then go on to The Pathway. That she and Dunsand were *people* with feelings never entered your head, did it? You were as careless of his as of hers. That Mrs Tate was in the habit of preparing for him on these occasions a special meal of his favourite food, of bringing good wine and beautiful flowers—to fill the void?—didn't trouble you at all. You told Dawn anything would do, just some quick picnic food for you and her to share. Any old wine, the cheapest she could get.

'She must go there first, you told her, and you gave her the key Mr Dunsand had sent to Mrs Tate and which Mrs Tate had given you. No responsibility, Mrs Tate? You left it all to Zeno?' Wexford turned back to Vedast. 'You'd be along around half past six. As soon as she was in the house she was to go upstairs where she would find a red dress.

'Now this dress had been laid out on the bed by Mr Dunsand. During his married life this dress of Mrs Tate's had been his favourite. When she wore it, sat down to dinner with him, listened to his account of his day and gave him account of hers, he could fancy himself protected from the "harsh light of day" and back safe and happy with his wife.

'Dawn knew nothing of this. She was told nothing of this. You asked her to wear this dress because it belonged to a fashion current when you were still together, still lovers, and you told her it would recall to you that past time.'

Looking ill, the colour all gone from his face, leaving a swarthy pallor, Tate lurched to his feet. He edged round the sofa and said to Vedast, 'Is that true?'

'We didn't mean any harm.'

'No harm? Christ . . . You did that and *she* knew it. God, I feel like I've never known either of you, never seen you before . . .'

'Godfrey . . .' Nell put out a feeble hand. 'I didn't do anything. I only told him—well, you know.'

'Have another drink, Goffo,' Vedast drawled.

'I don't want any more.' Tate made this remark in a thick but wondering voice. He swung on Wexford. 'Go on, then. What happened? Tell me the rest. Him . . .' He pointed at

Vedast as if reluctant to use his name. 'Him and her, they were with me that evening. Honest, they were. They can't have killed her.'

'Who kills, Mr Tate, the one who holds the knife, the one who says "stab!" or the one who sends the victim to the appointed place? Which of the three Fates is responsible for our destinies, she who spins the thread, she who cuts it or she who merely holds the scissors?' Wexford could tell from Tate's puzzled, vacant expression that all this was going over his head. 'Maybe Mr Dunsand could tell us. He's the philosopher.' Glancing at Burden, hoping there would be no actual exclamation of shock, he said, 'He killed her, of course. He's admitted it. He isn't the kind of man to prevaricate for long. Only chivalry made him tell a few lies to avoid any involvement of . . .' Scornful eyes came to rest on Nell, '. . . of his beloved former wife.'

Wexford went on carefully, 'As to what he did, I'll tell you. He came home, longing, of course, for the evening and the night ahead. He let himself in with his own key at twenty to seven. By that time Dawn must have been feeling uneasy. There were many things to make her uneasy, the modest size of the place, the austere furnishings, the superabundance of learned books. And the dress—a dress that was too small for her, unbecoming, too tight. Of course she felt uneasy. Of course, when she heard a key in the lock, she came out of the living room shyly, not speaking, just standing there.

'Instead of Vedast, she saw a little middle-aged stranger. Instead of his wife, Dunsand saw—what? What, Mrs Tate?'

'Dawn Stonor,' she said in a small, sullen voice.

'Oh, no. She didn't exist for him. He never even knew her name. He saw his wife, yet not his wife, a girl of his wife's age but bigger, coarser, with even more make-up, with brassier hair, yet wearing his wife's dress, his favourite dress.

'Perhaps he didn't believe in the reality of this sight. Even to a better-balanced man than Dunsand, what he saw looming

187

in the little hall would have seemed a hallucination. To him it wasn't just a travesty of his wife but a kind of succubus sent by something which existed in his clever sick mind to torment him. He wanted to destroy what he saw and he simply did so, attacking the hallucinatory shape with the first weapon that came to hand, the wine bottle his visitant had left on the hall table.'

Vedast got up, lifted his head sharply as he had lifted it at the festival, shook back his lion's mane. 'How was I to know things would go that way?' He held out his glass. 'Get me some more of that stuff, will you, Goffo.'

Tate said, 'Not me. Get your own bloody drink.'

'Temper, temper.' The golden eyebrows went up, the teeth showed in what was perhaps a smile.

'Can't you do anything to him?' Tate said to Wexford. 'He killed her. He's the real killer.'

'I know it, Mr Tate, but no, I can't do anything to him. What should be done to him? He is as sick as Mr Dunsand, a megalomaniac who lives on fantasies.'

'Don't give me that balls. He ought to be shot. Hanging'd be too good for him.'

' "Heaven hath no rage like love to hatred turned" . . . You are not obliged to associate with them, Mr Tate. You need not, just because you also married her, copy her first husband and be chivalrous.'

'Too bloody right, I needn't.' Shock had brought Tate complete cold sobriety. On his knees, he flung armfuls of garments into the red grip, seized it and a smaller suitcase. 'I'm going, I'm quitting.' He got up, said to Vedast, 'You owe me a hundred quid. You can send it care of my mum's. *She* knows the address.'

'You can't go,' said Vedast and at last he wasn't playing. His voice had lost its lightness. 'We've been together for eight years. What'll I do without you?'

'Cut your bloody throat, but cut hers first.' Tate held out his hand to Wexford. 'I used to call you lot pigs,' he said, 'and maybe I will again. But, thanks, you've done me a good turn. If you've done nothing else you've got me away from them. I might even stop drinking now.' Then he used the first cultivated, literate phrase Wexford had ever heard from his lips but, even as he said it, the chief inspector knew he had learnt it parrot fashion from the 'scene' with which he had been associated. 'They'd have destroyed me utterly.'

'I really think they would, Mr Tate.'

When he had gone, slamming the suite door, the slave who remained seized Vedast's arm and said, 'Good riddance. I just feel relief, don't you?'

Vedast made no reply. He picked up the phone sullenly, asked for a porter. Immediately Nell, taking her cue, bundled heaps of clothes into cases, bags, carriers. Wexford and Burden, ready to leave, helpless, impotent, watched her. The cases were all packed in five minutes. Vedast stood at the window, his expression inscrutable. He looked over the balcony rail once, perhaps at the departing Tate. The porter came in, took two cases in his hands, one under his arm. Nell flung a white coat round her shoulders.

'I take it we shan't be wanted any more?'

'You will be wanted at Mr Dunsand's trial. Before that, statements will have to be taken from you.'

'Me?' said Vedast. 'I can't appear in court. It will be ghastly bad publicity. Why did Goffo have to go like that? Goffo could have coped.'

'I'll cope,' said Nell fondly. 'Let's go now, shall we? It's nearly midnight. Let's get going.'

He pushed her away. 'I'm going,' he said. 'I'm going by myself. You can get a taxi to whatever station there is in this hole.'

'But we've got the car!'

Petulantly, like a little boy, he said, 'It's my car. *I'm* going in it. You'd better face it, Nello, you're no use to me without Godfrey. He looked after me and then—then you came along.' His face cleared a little. 'You were a nice bit of decoration,' he said.

The flesh of her face seemed to sag. Her lip curled up, her eyes widened, stretching the skin, wrinkling it. 'You can't mean it, Zeno. Zeno, don't leave me! I've worshipped you since I was twenty. I've never thought of any man but you.'

'No, dear, I know. You just married them.'

As the porter returned to fetch the remaining luggage, Vedast tried to unhook her hands from his shoulders. 'Nello, do as I say. Let go of me. I'm going to pay the bill and then I'm going.' He went up to Wexford, the bantering tone quelled by what he had to say and by the presence of the inquisitive porter. 'I suppose we can keep all this quiet?' One of the long, lean hands sketched a gesture towards a jeans pocket. 'I imagine...'

'Mr Vedast, we are leaving.'

'I'll come down with you.'

'Zeno!' Nell screamed. 'Zeno, I love you!'

The two policemen had moved a pace or two away from the singer, moved distastefully. Nell flung herself upon Vedast. Her coat fell from her shoulders. She clung to his neck, pushing her fingers through the golden hair, pressing her body against him.

'Where am I to go? What am I to do?'

Struggling, pushing her, he said, 'You can go to Godfrey's mum. Go where you like, only get off me. Get off! Christ, Dawn Stonor'd have been a better bet than you. Get off!'

They grappled together like wrestlers, Nell screaming and clinging. Vedast was strong and muscular but not quite strong enough. He kicked and punched, grabbing at her hair, tearing it. They toppled and rolled on the floor among the dead flowers, the empty bottles, knocking over and breaking into fragments the orange-juice glass.

'Let's go,' said Wexford laconically.

In the corridor bedroom doors had been cautiously opened and sleepy people stared out. On the stairs the policemen passed four or five of the hotel night staff running up, alarmed by the screams, the thumps on the floorboards. Lights began to come on as the somnolent hotel woke to life.

The night was as clear, as softly violet-blue as the night of the festival, but now the moon was waning. And there were no ballads to be heard here, no plangent note from a string plucked with controlled power. Wexford could still hear Vedast's voice, though, raised now in a high-pitched lunatic scream, a sound none of his fans would have recognised. Instead of that vibrant twang came the crash of flying furniture; instead of melody, Nell's hysterical sobbing, and instead of applause, the manager gravely and quite ineffectively begging his guests to stop.

'Perhaps they'll kill each other,' said Burden as they passed the furred golden car.

'Perhaps they will. Who cares?' Wexford sighed. 'Vedast won't like it in court. Will it have any effect on his career?'

Once again Burden was being appealed to as the expert on such matters. 'I doubt it,' he said, starting the car. 'These singers, they're always appearing in court on drug offences. Did you ever hear of their records selling less well afterwards?'

'Drugs are one thing. Provided you don't deal in them, drugs harm no one but yourself. But there's a big thing among young people at the moment for loving your neighbour, for not hurting—above all, for keeping in mind that people are people. I don't think they'll be too pleased when they know their idol forgot or, rather, neglected to care for that fact.'

'Poor old Dunsand. What of him?'

'His career will be ruined, but it won't be prison for him. Mental hospital for years? Is that much better? It was a succubus he killed. Unfortunately for him, we know succubi don't exist—they're flesh and blood.'

A single light showed in Burden's bungalow. In an armchair in the living room John lay asleep, his hair tousled, a half-empty glass of milk beside him. The indicator light on the record player still glowed red.

'God, I forgot the kids! I was so carried away I forgot them.' Burden stooped tenderly over his son, but the boy didn't stir. 'He waited up for me,' he said wonderingly.

Wexford smiled rather sadly. 'Poor John. Somehow I don't think he'll get the Sundays album for his birthday now.'

'He certainly won't.' Burden took a stride to the record player, his face flushing with anger when he saw what lay on the turntable. Savagely, he seized 'Let-me-believe' in both hands and seemed about to twist it, to bend it double, when Wexford laid a gentle, warning hand on his arm.

'No, Mike,' he said. 'Don't do that. Leave it to John and—and all of them. Let them be his judges.'